Open Lens

A novel

Lisa Buffaloe

Open Lens

John 15:11 Publications
Copyright 2022 Lisa Brewer Buffaloe (updated 071423)

Visit the author's website at https://lisabuffaloe.com

ISBN 978-1-957715-01-8 (eBook)
ISBN 978-1-957715-02-5 (Paperback)
ISBN 978-1-957715-03-2 (Hardcover)

Cover design: Lisa Buffaloe

Printed in the United States of America

Open Lens

*May the eyes of your heart be enlightened to
know... Ephesians 1:18*

**As the eyes of the heart open,
what truths will be revealed?**

Although Alyssa Nelson chose nursing for her profession, she hasn't found a cure for her broken heart. Photographing nature in her off-hours takes her mind off her pain. However, the photos she captures in her camera's memory card can't replace the memory of her heartache and regrets.

When Alyssa comes face-to-face with her past, she is thrown into police investigations, mystery, intrigue, and a touch of fun.

The truth comes into focus as Alyssa's heart opens to God's healing, yet will she make the same mistakes she made before, or will she choose a new beginning?

One

Ice blocks, naked rears, and drunk frat boys do not mix. Alyssa Nelson chuckled as she walked down the hospital corridor. Living in a college town made the times she worked in the emergency room night shift rather interesting. Several fraternity guys had decided to ride ice blocks down a large hill outside of town.

To top off their interesting outing, one of them decided to go au-natural. After his not-so-brilliant move, his friends brought him and his bright-red rear to the hospital's emergency room. Frostbite wasn't a problem, but the guy would have a heck of a rash from skidding the last third of the hill on his bare derriere.

Alyssa turned the corner and waved to her friend, Victoria, who worked in the cafeteria. "Good morning!"

"Hey, cute thing, how was your shift?" Victoria wiped off a table then pushed chairs back into place. Although Victoria was a grandmother, she still turned heads. Her outward appearance shined from her caring smile and friendliness that always saw the best in others.

Alyssa grinned and walked toward her

friend. "The ER is never boring."

"You had ER duty overnight? You sure are chipper for working there; you're usually dragging." Victoria resumed her position behind the cash register and handed Alyssa a large to-go cup.

"The usual stress was there until a few hours ago. Then...well, let's just say college guys have amusing ideas."

"Girlfriend, I had way too much fun in college. I could tell stories that would make your hair stand on end. Fortunately, life calmed down once I started dating my husband."

"How long have you been married?"

Victoria beamed, her gaze lingering on the small diamond on her ring finger. "Thirty-three years this month."

Alyssa smiled at her friend. "Good for you." After paying for her purchase, she walked over to pour her coffee and add a healthy dose of cream and sugar.

"We've had some great times and raised some wonderful kids." Victoria held up her hand and hurried toward the kitchen area. "Let me get you a shot of whip cream. Don't want you to go out into the cold, cruel world without the proper needs for survival."

"Thanks. I'm heading to the Payette river to take photos." With any luck, she'd get that perfect shot as early-morning clouds radiated a delicious rainbow color.

Sam, working at the grill, bobbed his bald

head to greet Alyssa. "Hey, stop by in the next few days; I'd love to see your latest photos. I've got my drone working again if you'd like to use it sometime."

"That'd be great. Maybe we can get together soon, and you can fly the camera up for some new angles." She'd be a world-renowned photographer if people appreciated her pictures like Sam did. Sure, she'd won a few contests in the area and even sold her prints at craft fairs during summer months, but not enough to provide a living.

Whip cream canister in hand, Victoria stopped in front of Alyssa. "Make sure you eat breakfast."

Alyssa gave her friend a mock curtsy. "Yes, ma'am. I have a cinnamon roll in my car."

"I guess that'll do." Victoria swirled a shot of white froth onto Alyssa's coffee. "I've got to keep you healthy. You still haven't met my youngest son."

"I'm sure he's great, but I'm happy being on my own." Her broken heart was not ready for a rematch.

"Right." Victoria's head-tilt said more than her comment.

"There are tons of positives to being single." Alyssa straightened her shoulders. "I don't need a man. I'll just get a Beta fish."

"I tell you, you need to meet my son. Jerry's a keeper."

"The one in Coeur d'Alene? He doesn't even

live here."

"He'll be back. And when he returns, he'll need a good woman like you. He said he'd like to meet you."

"Oh, please. You didn't tell him you wanted him to meet someone with a great personality, did you?"

"You *do* have a great personality."

"Ugh. That's like telling a guy I'm ugly as sin."

From the kitchen, Sam looked up with sympathy in his eyes and responded with a knowing nod.

Victoria took Alyssa by the arm and led her to the cash register. "It is not. I told him you were pretty too, and I know he likes red heads. With your gorgeous strawberry-blond hair and your great personality, he won't have a chance."

"Did you tell him I was pretty first or a good personality first?"

"I don't know. What does it matter? You are pretty with a great personality."

Alyssa sighed and took a sip of her deliciously cream-laced coffee. "Thank you, but no thank you. I have a date with a sunrise."

Victoria's hand settled lightly on Alyssa's arm. "God has someone special in mind for that heart of yours."

Though Victoria's comment made Alyssa's chest ache with longing, she smiled and raised her cup. "Yeah, well, things haven't gone too well so far."

Turning down the hallway, she quickened her pace. If all went well, she'd spend an hour playing outside, then be home in time to say hello to her roomie, catch some shut eye, and then go back to work the night shift again at the hospital. Not much social life, but work and photographing nature did leave her somewhat happy and fulfilled.

Maybe she'd end up shuffling around like a happy little spinster. The dull pain in her heart discontinued that thought.

In the parking lot, Alyssa buckled herself in the seatbelt of her SUV. Boise traffic would begin building soon as people started their day. Snow had fallen in the hills, and if she timed it right, maybe a few icicles would sparkle when the morning sun made its appearance.

Alyssa turned her vehicle north on Highway 55 toward Horseshoe Bend. The Payette river journeyed alongside the road, and one particular spot had a great place to take pictures of the sunrise. Or at least what could be seen after the sun made its way over the hills.

Reaching her destination, Alyssa waited for traffic to clear, u-turned, and pulled her SUV onto the shoulder next to the river.

She drew her hood over her head and bundled up, making sure every part except her eyes were covered from the winter cold. By the time she had on her gear, she was practically bulletproof.

Camera in hand and backpack slung over

her shoulder, Alyssa stepped out of the car. A truck going way too fast zoomed past and blasted her with cold air. She shivered and hurried down to the river until she reached the sand bar. Air, crisp and clean, filled her lungs as she sat on a large boulder.

Working as a floating nurse had challenges. Some nights she'd be in the Emergency Room; other times, she'd help out on different floors, wherever the hospital said she was most needed. She liked the variety and the opportunity to encounter various people, but it limited her friendships and certainly limited her love life. Plus, none of her day-shift friends had any interest in getting up at the crack of dawn.

However, early, cold mornings afforded the luxury of no human visitors—just her and nature. The solitude was pleasant, healing, a form of freedom to be alone ... sometimes.

Trying to ignore the empty gnawing in her chest, she concentrated on the soothing sounds of water gliding and tumbling over rocks made visible by winter's drop in water levels.

The sky began the gradual change from midnight blue. Fortunately, a few clouds in the atmosphere could reflect whatever colors the sun would provide. Waiting, Alyssa readied her camera.

In seconds the symphony of color began. A melon tint painted the clouds above the hills. Perfectly framing the shot, she caught the reflection off the water up to the sky. The click of her shutter captured photos as God's glory played in the clouds.

~~~

Sean Connery sighed and focused on the runway as he taxied the private jet for departure. He'd heard every joke in the book about his name. The ladies sitting in the back of the plane were probably still laughing. At least this plane had a private cockpit where he could keep some level of privacy.

Mark, his co-pilot, cast a sympathetic gaze toward Sean. "Most guys would love to have a name like yours, but man, those women sure did make some suggestive comments."

Sean nodded. "It definitely has had challenges." Trying to be a good guy with the name of someone who made the movie character James Bond legendary wasn't always easy. Some days he didn't mind having a famous name, but today it just made him lonely.

Finally cleared for takeoff, Sean accelerated the Gulfstream to full speed, waited for liftoff, and then soared into the sky. The plane's flaps were raised, wheels retracted, and Sean set his heading and climbed to the proper altitude.

Being in the sky, above the world, gave a sense of peace and freedom.

Dance music played in the back, and a party started. He'd made far too many mistakes in the past, and he was determined to live differently now. The women he flew in their private jets wanted him to be anything but decent, while the woman he really wanted only saw him as a friend.

Two

Three o'clock in the afternoon, camera bag strapped across his shoulder, Tom Chambers exited the plane at the Boise, Idaho airport. Even if he couldn't afford first class, the six thousand bucks he'd spent on his equipment had been worth every penny.

He wheeled his carry-on luggage to the rental car counter.

A cute redhead greeted him. "Are you a professional photographer?"

"Sure am."

She smiled and fluttered her eyelashes. "I'm taking Creative Photography at Boise State." Her hair, petite stature, and innocent smile reminded him of his college girlfriend. Strange, he hadn't thought about her in years.

Tom responded to the clerk with a smile. "Nice."

She grinned. "Most people just use their camera cell phones to take pictures and don't care about the professional quality of photos. Do you find that's true?"

Tom nodded. "There will always be a need for the pros. If photography is your passion, go for it." If he weren't on a rushed timetable, he'd turn on the charm and see if anything developed. But, to make sure he arrived at his destination before dark, he kept the chat light and hurried to his rental.

Buckling in the car, Tom's excitement grew. He'd been paid upfront for the job with actress Emily Kingston. The more her photos appeared in front of the public, the higher her box-office draw. The camera loved Emily. She had the "it" quality and turned heads wherever she went.

Behind that sexy exterior, he'd found something sweet and unique. The last two weeks, she'd been out of the limelight. Some claimed she'd burnt out on the Hollywood lifestyle and was in hiding, but Tom knew where she was. He checked his GPS and set it for his destination.

Beyond the Boise area, the drive would take a few hours to get to his assignment. Enjoying the view of the mountainous countryside, his thoughts turned back to Emily. Three weeks ago, he'd met her in a coffee shop. The actress wanted to thank him for how his photographs always showed her in the best light. Emily even asked about his work and seemed genuinely interested in everything about him.

Time with her had been surreal as they'd talked about their lives, hopes, and dreams. Emily, even though a sexy knockout, had a sweetness about her. She shared with him about the positives and negatives of being considered a star, the craziness of some of her fans, and that she'd even received a few death threats.

Being a photographer in Hollywood, Tom understood the wild side of fame. Just last week, he'd fought off a guy who tried to take his camera to get the photos he'd taken of a star leaving a downtown club. Yet, with all the madness of the Hollywood lifestyle, someone like Emily made it all worthwhile.

Emily had even been open enough to say she had trouble sleeping, that she would turn on all the lights and walk the floor at night. He'd probably do the same after watching her last suspense-thriller blockbuster and what she shared about her weird fans. With a quiver in her voice, she'd asked what Tom would do if he ever saw someone attacked. When he saw the fear in her eyes, it took all his strength not to reach out and hold her close. For someone like Emily, he'd fight to the death.

No telling what would have happened if they had met under different circumstances. Shame she was involved with her boyfriend, slime, David, aka producer, director, actor, and total jerk. What she saw in him, Tom would never understand.

Hours later, Tom stood on the hill overlooking Emily Kingston's cabin. His breath hovered and crystallized in the night air. Snow crunched under his feet as he stamped to return the feeling in his toes.

Cold air's icy fingers seeped down his jacket, and he flipped up his jacket collar. Bright stars dotted the sky, and in the cabin below, Emily slept. He checked through the camera's viewfinder and waited. Tonight, he'd get the perfect shot.

A lamp near the window switched on, a soft glow illuminating the den. Emily, dressed in a nightgown, her long blond hair cascading around her shoulders, walked to the kitchen, poured herself a drink, then came back and stood at the window looking out as though she could see him.

How he longed to be with her, to hold her close, but what chance did a mere photographer have with a girl like her?

Then again, maybe this would be his opportunity.

Three

Five hours into her night shift, Alyssa stopped in her tracks as the hospital code system signaled urgency. She turned and hurried to put on a gown, gloves, and glasses, then took her place among the respiratory specialists, attending and resident doctors, nurses, and emergency service assistants.

The patient flown in by the Life Flight helicopter was moved to a hospital stretcher. As the paramedic reported details -- motor vehicle accident, one car, unconscious at the scene, forearm fracture, punctured lung, rib fracture, broken kneecap, ACL tear -- Alyssa's gaze rested on the patient.

Hands worked to stabilize him as doctors and nurses assessed the damage, took vital signs, and documented findings on the trauma flow sheet. The trauma nurse started intravenous access to administer fluids, medications, and blood products.

Glass strewn in his brown hair glistened in the light. His bruised and swollen face was covered in blood from a gash running along his cheek marred his handsome face. Something about the man seemed familiar.

And then, Alyssa knew...

Four

Shift over, Alyssa closed her townhouse door, laid her purse on the counter, and walked to the medicine cabinet in the bathroom. After all these years, she couldn't believe Tom Chambers was here in Idaho, and still, the heart pain lingered.

He obviously hadn't come searching for her. Why had he been out in the mountains? If someone hadn't called 911, he would never have survived.

The ache in her chest wouldn't go away. Why did she still have feelings for him? They had dated all through college, but the last two weeks before college graduation, he'd avoided her like the plague, never called, and never returned her calls. She should never, ever, *ever*, have allowed herself to get involved with him. Not that she was a saint or anything, but there was something about that first love. She grabbed antacids and popped two.

"Hey."

Alyssa turned at the sound of her roommate's voice.

"What's up with you?" Katarina brushed her long, dark hair as she walked to Alyssa and stopped within inches of her face. "You're oozing negative vibes."

"Sorry." Alyssa avoided her roommate's questioning violet eyes and stepped back from her annoying habit of being way too perceptive. "Someone I knew was brought into the ER. Life flight"

"Ouch. Are they going to pull through?"

Alyssa nodded. "He's a mess, but he'll be okay." A pang of guilt surfaced for being so mad at Tom, but she promptly squashed it down. The guy deserved a good beating for what he did to her. Okay, maybe not that bad a beating.

"He?" Katrina stopped her brushing.

"Yes. He. Someone I knew from college."

"Really? Someone special?"

"No ... Yes ... No. Definitely not." Alyssa fingered the antacids. She'd been young, naïve, and easily led astray by Tom's boyish charm. When they met her freshman year, they'd had a couple of drinks, some dancing, and in her weak and stupid state, she believed his lie that he loved her. He played the part so well, and for most of their time together, their relationship seemed a match to last forever. But right before graduation, everything changed—including him.

"Care to explain?" Katarina took the antacid container from Alyssa and returned it to the cabinet.

"His name is Tom Chambers. We dated in college." Alyssa walked to the kitchen and took a water bottle from the refrigerator.

Katrina followed. "Oh, *that* guy. Star crossed lovers meet again. Sounds like the makings of a good movie."

"More like a horror flick."

"Oh, come on, he couldn't be that bad."

"He took my heart and ran it through a paper shredder."

"Ouch. Guess Tom won't be getting top-notch care from his nursing staff."

"I didn't tell anyone."

Kat gave her a gentle hug. "I'm sorry he hurt you."

Alyssa accepted the embrace, then pressed the bridge of her nose, willing away any moisture that might dare escape from her eyes. "I thought I was over him."

Kat gazed at the ceiling and sighed. "Love is an emotion that wells and aches within our souls not quenched by time and space." She then took Alyssa's hands. "May I use your emotions? I'm working on another poem for our poetry group. One of those long-lost, unrequited love-type things. The timings great."

Alyssa shrugged. "Sure. I guess so." Kat's poetry group had more men than women. Alyssa had gone once and sat amazed as the guys sat on the edge of their seats for each of Kat's readings. No matter what was said, the reactions were always highly positive. Disgustingly so. Kat could have a date every night if she wanted and probably hadn't paid for her own meal since childhood.

Her roommate hugged her again. "I'll give you full credit for anything I use."

"That's okay. Take it, run with it. I'll make sure I tell you anything that might be useful." At least someone would get use out of her negative emotions.

"You're the best. I better get to work." Kat turned, and her black hair swayed with her cat-like walk as she headed to the door.

Alyssa contemplated another antacid since she hadn't had an actual date in six months. Not that she hadn't been asked—mainly by drunks who staggered into the ER, or frat boys, even a doctor or two—who, unfortunately, were married. The guy from the lab had been a nice distraction last year and even for a short time looked promising, but no one could come close to the emotions she'd felt for Tom.

After that relationship, she should have become a nun and signed up for a convent or run off and joined some humanitarian organization in a foreign country. She would have thought Idaho would have been far enough. Most people just thought the state was a potato patch. Few people knew about the incredible beauty.

Her roommate bundled her coat and put her gloves on over her long, slender fingers. Black pants and a tight black sweater, just low enough to draw attention without revealing too much, covered her five-foot-seven-inch frame. No matter what the weather or where she was going, Kat looked like she stepped out of the pages of a fashion magazine.

Alyssa went to the couch, slumped down, and pulled a throw pillow to her chest. "See you at dinner?"

"Sorry, not tonight. I'm going out with Stephen." Kat said the guy's name like he was a luscious dessert. "We might even see that new action movie."

"Stephen ... the lawyer? Blonde, hunky, six-foot-four lawyer?"

"He's only six foot three, but you did get the rest correct. He is a hunk." Kat tilted her head in contemplation, then sat next to Alyssa and patted her hand like she was a little girl. "You've got to get out more. I know you work nights, but maybe we could find you some gorgeous man who is off during the daylight hours like you are."

"I'm fine."

"I worry about you. Tell you what. Next night when you have off, we'll do something together and have a girl's night out. Or we'll stay here and watch some romantic comedy in our PJs." Kat nudged her. "Come on, give me a smile."

Alyssa responded with a shrug.

"Well, that's not great, but will have to do. I'm going to be late. Chin up. Life will get better." When Alyssa didn't respond, Kat stood and draped a blanket from the back of the couch over Alyssa's shoulders. "Get some rest.

Things will look better after some sleep."

After Kat left, Alyssa didn't want to think or remember. She curled into a ball and closed her eyes, yet every thought drifted to Tom.

Somewhere between reminiscing about her college days and her lost hopes and dreams about Tom, finally, sleep came.

Jolting at the sound of her ringing cell phone, Alyssa squinted at the display and checked the caller. Seeing the name of her childhood friend on caller-id made her smile. She struggled to sit up and pressed to answer. "Hey."

"Got time to see your favorite pilot?" Sean's deep voice brought comfort.

"Are you in town?"

"Flew in about an hour ago, and I'm looking for an early dinner date. My treat."

Alyssa threw off the cover. "Give me half an hour, and I'll be ready." Sean was one guy she always enjoyed seeing. Who wouldn't want to have a date with Sean Connery?

"I'll be there."

Smiling, she hurried to take a quick shower. Sean was the one she could personally thank for leading her into the medical profession. His parents had been obsessed with anything James Bond. Poor Sean had to play tough and be tough. He tried to live up to his name and did things most boys wouldn't dare.

Two years older, Alyssa took the role of a friend and nurse for his daredevil antics. Since she lived across the street, she'd baby him, pat him on the shoulder, and even kiss him on the cheek before sending him back home.

One day, Sean jumped from the house's roof to his mom's SUV as she backed out of the garage. That stunt did not go as planned. He wound up with a broken arm, sprained ankle, and a broken nose. The blood volume required a call to an ambulance and a trip to the hospital.

When two handsome paramedics showed up to take care of Sean, one had squeezed Alyssa on the shoulder and thanked her for her help. From that day forward, she wanted to work in a hospital.

Alyssa put on fresh makeup and took another look in the mirror before slipping on her shoes and darting to the door. Sean always arrived on time.

At the sound of the doorbell, she opened the door and blinked. When did he get so handsome and so tall? She shook off the thought. Their relationship had always been friends, more like brother and sister.

"Connery." He smiled and leaned his six-foot frame against the door. His blond hair, which he always kept short, now had a touch of a spike at the front. His otherwise perfect nose tilted just a smidgen to the right. "Sean Connery at your service."

"You nut." She shoved him out of the way and locked the door behind her. "Long time no see, Mr. Connery."

"Six months. But who's counting. And, phone calls do not count."

She followed him to his rental. "You have better things to do than think of me."

"Alyssa, dear." Sean opened her car door and turned on the actor charm with an authentic Sean Connery accent. "No one can replace you."

"Give me a break." She slipped into the car seat and looked up at him. "How many women have you dated during those six months?"

His bluish-gray eyes surveyed her with a little-boy innocent look he did so well. "Not more than a dozen." He cocked an eyebrow, grinned, and closed her door.

For some reason, today, that bothered her. Of course, they were just friends. Friends for fifteen years through childhood, the mutant pre-teen years, bike rides to the pond for fishing, wading in the little stream that ran behind their neighborhood, watching the stars in the evenings, wondering who they would be once they got older.

He buckled in his seat and leaned toward her, way too close, or perhaps not close enough. "So, how many men have you dated?" His clean smell permeated her senses.

No way she would say zero. She tossed her head, hopefully feigning a mysterious air. "Wouldn't you like to know?"

With a smile, he started the car. "I love it when you're coy." He placed his right hand on her headrest as he turned to look over his shoulder to back into the street. "What sounds good?"

"How about Mongolian?"

"My favorite."

At this time of day, they had the restaurant to themselves. They chose a booth then went to the long salad bar filled with veggies and meats. She took the smallest bowl and charted her path, making sure to get her favorites in before her bowl filled to the brim.

She glanced at Sean. How could he get so much stuffed in a bowl without food exploding over the sides?

Alyssa surveyed her choices. Before she handed it to the cook, she still needed to dip a few of the best sauces for cooking – ginger, chef's special, peanut sauce, garlic, and a few others.

The cook placed their ingredients on a vast, round, flat heated surface, then moved their food along with a bamboo stick as it cooked. A few times around the sizzling top and everything was perfectly prepared and placed in new bowls.

Show over and food ready, Alyssa followed Sean back to their seats. "So, where have you been in your latest adventures?"

"I flew in to drop off a few clients and have a couple of days to rest and relax. You were the first person I thought of."

"Thanks. However, I'm the only person you

know in this part of Idaho."

"True, but no one else is as fun either. In all my travels, I haven't met anyone else who had Shultzy, Gertrude, and Roosevelt."

"I can't believe you still remember my pet's names." Alyssa got a touch misty-eyed, remembering her long ago fur babies. Her family's two wiener dogs—Shultzy and Gertrude, along with their cat.

"You miss them?"

"I do. They were so much fun." With all her doctoring, the poor pups became quite the hypochondriacs by the time they got older. The cat, Roosevelt Franklin, was one cool cat. Roosevelt had enough weight on him; he'd lay in the yard and wait for an unsuspecting dog to dare step paw into his domain. The cat wouldn't move, would just lay sphinxlike, watching. And, if a dog got close enough, Roosevelt would lunge, grab the dog by the shoulders, and flip him on his back. The dogs never knew what hit them. Plus, anytime Roosevelt would get in fights during nights of catting around, he'd hobble over to the vet that lived down the street to bandage his wounds.

Sean nudged her foot, bringing her back from her thoughts. "You should get a puppy."

"I'm not home enough for a puppy."

"Even more reason to get one. Get something that grows big that you can take when you go out on your photoshoots."

Alyssa twirled her fork through her noodles.

"It would be too hard to photograph while babysitting an animal."

"I'm talking about a well-trained dog." Sean rubbed at his chin as though thinking deep thoughts. "Maybe I'll ask some of my clients. Someone might have a dog needing a new home." He grinned. "Or, you could get a little one and strap it on your backpack and outfit the little guy in a Harley biker outfit."

"Oh yeah, that would scare off any attacker."

"Probably would work; they'd be so distracted by your little brute; you'd have plenty of time to get away. Really, I think you should get a big dog. Maybe a Labrador. They're loyal and trainable."

"Your clients probably have little purebreds they dress up in outfits and fit in their expensive purses."

"Some do, but you're smarter than the women I fly around who don't think anything of dropping a few thousand on a day shopping trip."

"I bet you've had some interesting propositions."

Sean took a bite of his food and munched for a few moments. "Interesting, but not appealing. I don't want to lose my job, and I don't want to lose my self-respect."

"So, you don't live like your name-sake? Most guys wouldn't talk so openly about their lack of conquests." The thought made her smile.

"I don't tell everyone. Actually, you're the only one who knows. Maybe people feel freer to talk around their medical providers."

"Gee, thanks. That's all I am, a medical provider?"

"Hey, I haven't asked you for a bandage since you went off to college and left me alone bleeding with gushing wounds." Sean sat straight and puffed his chest. "But it made me a man."

"If I remember correctly, you didn't need my services once you got your pilot license. I might have left for college, but you flew away."

His grin combined with the rise of one eyebrow. "Why Ms. Alyssa, I do believe you noticed. But alas, the air always called to me."

"That's probably why you had so many bumps and bruises. You were always jumping off of something. Probably a good thing you have to strap yourself in when you fly."

He nodded toward the window. "If it was warmer, we could go skydiving."

"No, thank you. I'm fine here on the ground."

"You always were the grounded one." Sean smiled, placed money on the table for the tip, and grabbed the check before she could. "Do you have time for a movie or dessert?"

Alyssa checked her watch; she needed more sleep before her shift started. A few more hours, and she would see Tom again. Her fun with Sean nose-dived into an antacid-inducing bellyache. "I better get back home."

Concern etched Sean's face. "You okay?"

"Yep." She mustered up a smile. "Just never know what a night at the hospital will bring." She'd check on Tom and maybe find out what happened between them before college graduation. Had she done something wrong? Why did he stop loving her? She searched through her purse, looking for another antacid.

"You sure you're okay?"

She avoided looking his way and popped an antacid. "Yeah, just stuff."

"You know I'm always here for you." His deep voice made her heartache in ways she hadn't felt in a long time.

Once they arrived at her townhouse, Alyssa glanced at Sean as he walked her to the door. "I'd ask you in, but I don't have long before my shift starts." She needed more time to contemplate what to say to Tom and whether or not she should slap him or hug him.

"No problem." Sean rested his hand on the doorframe above her head as she unlocked her door. "I'm staying in the hotel on the river in Eagle. Got time for me tomorrow?"

"Sure, I was going to see if I could get some photos of the river after my shift. Want to come? It would be pretty early" Alyssa gazed up at Sean. Why did everyone have to be taller? Even in heels, she'd barely reach his shoulder.

He nodded. "What time?"

"I get off at 6:00 in the morning. I hope that's not too early." When did his shoulders get that broad? She swallowed to bring back moisture to her dry throat. "Want to meet me at the hospital? We can drive from there." Her voice squeaked.

He grinned and shoved his hands in his jean's pockets. "It's not too early. I'll be there."

She closed the door but peeked through the peephole to watch as he walked away. They had years of history between them and so many good times; why wouldn't she consider something more?

Sighing, she turned away.

Five

Attempting to open his eyes, Tom tried to concentrate as pain slithered from his every pore. Everything hurt, which included his eyelashes. Finally successful, light filtered in. Where was he? He struggled to focus, but everything remained fuzzy. Beeping came from his left, antiseptic smells filtered through his nose. Was he in a hospital?

A noise sounded from his right -- shuffling papers, a chair creaked, and footsteps came closer. "Mr. Chambers, I need to ask you some questions regarding Emily Kingston." The deep voice came from next to him.

He could make out the big man wore a uniform. A policeman? Memories flooded back from Emily. He swallowed, trying to dislodge the fuzz in his throat. "Is she okay?"

"What do you remember?"

Tom tried to push himself up, but his arms wouldn't work. He craned his neck, which only brought extreme pain and a bout of nauseating dizziness. Groaning, he stilled himself and closed his eyes, and remembered.

Emily standing in the window. In the shadows behind her, a figure moved toward her.

Even from this distance, he swore he heard Emily's scream. His semi-numb fingers fumbled with the camera as he tried to zoom in on her attacker. The clicking of his shutter sounded like gunshots in the still air.

What was he thinking? She needed his help. He reached for his cell phone. No service. With one swipe, he grabbed his belongings, slipping and sliding as he ran to his car.

Desperate to get to Emily, he started the rental car's engine and stamped the accelerator. His vehicle fishtailed on the icy road leading to her cabin. Ahead of him on the road, his headlights illuminated a closed iron gate. Speeding faster, he braced for impact.

A sound drew him back to the painful present.

"I tried to get there. Somebody grabbed her."

"Who?" The big man loomed above him, his voice gruff. "What did you see?"

"I couldn't see... couldn't get there in time." Tom coughed and gagged.

The room spun and whirled. Blackness overtook.

Six

Alyssa rode the elevator to her favorite floor of the hospital. Besides the incredible view of the mountains and the city, most people in their care were pretty agreeable.

Working the night shift gave her the advantage since most patients slept—except for Mr. Jensen. He was every nurse's nightmare. After his latest surgery, he seemed to look for ways to torment those with who he came in contact. Since he was always awake, the staff had decided he was an old, irritable vampire. During the day, he hated his blinds open, and his dark, beady eyes watched every move when someone came into his room. Shuddering at the thought, she wished she'd worn the cross her grandmother had given her at college graduation. Thank goodness Mr. Jensen would move soon to rehab.

Alyssa followed the curved wall to the nurse's station. The head nurse, Carla, sat typing at the computer, her fingers moving at the speed of a hyperactive hummingbird. Fortunately, Carla was happy to help anyone with their computer paperwork if they brought her dessert. How someone who stood six feet, ate like a linebacker, yet could hide behind a walking cane, was the topic of many discussions in the lounge during breaks.

Carla glanced at Alyssa. "Glad you're with us tonight. How was life in the ER?"

"Crazy, sad, and sometimes fun." Alyssa checked over the night's information and schedule. Her heart screeched to a stop and rammed up her throat. Tom Chambers' room was down the hall. How did they move him so fast?

Computer clicks stopped. "Are you okay?" Carla was on her feet and by Alyssa's side in lightning speed. "You don't look good."

To steady herself, Alyssa leaned against the counter. "I'm alright, just some heartburn." Burnt to a crisp, heartburn. Why didn't she think about Tom being on her floor? She had planned on seeing him, but did she really want to see him?

"Do you need a chair?" Before Alyssa could decline, Carla wheeled over a desk chair and forced her to sit. "You're white as a bleached sheet."

The heat of embarrassment rose to her cheeks; Alyssa got to her feet and tried to look in control. "I'm okay."

"Well, your color did return. Maybe you need to have some blood work done. If you're feeling bad, go home. I can get a floater up on the floor tonight."

"Nah, I'll be fine. I'll walk it off during my

rounds." Alyssa pasted on a smile, retrieved her computer work cart, and made a quick exit in the opposite direction of Tom's room. She'd save him for last. Maybe he would be asleep, and she'd have time to compose herself. Unfortunately, that meant going first to Mr. Jensen's room.

She paused before entering, then stepped inside. The man's room was dark, and the television tuned to a news channel reporting the latest tragedies. His dinner remained on the tray in front of him; most of the food remained untouched.

She flipped on the light.

"Stupid nurse. Turn off that blasted light. You here to poke at me like the rest of them?"

"The light has to stay on for now. And yes, I'm here to make sure you're doing okay."

"If I were okay, I wouldn't be here."

She retrieved the blood-pressure cuff and stood next to his bed. "Knee surgery is tough, but you're progressing well. Soon you'll be running all over the place."

He huffed. "I did not run anywhere when I was young, and I am not about to start now. That's what employees are for. My family thinks I need to quit, but I plan on working until they wheel me out in a casket."

"You enjoy your work that much?"

"Enjoy? Who said anything about enjoy? Work is only a vehicle to make money."

She strapped on the cuff to his paper-thin

arm. "So, what do you do for fun?"

"Fun?" His piercing eyes slitted his displeasure. "Fun is for idiots."

"I guess I'm not too bright; I like to have fun."

He humphed and stared at his food tray.

Alyssa checked and recorded his vitals in the computer system and made a quick exit. After finishing the rest of her rounds, she stopped outside Tom's door. Two hundred and ten thousand butterflies somersaulted and assaulted her stomach.

For the last four years, she'd imagined what it would be like to see Tom again. Would they get back together and everything work out? If only she had a body like Katarina, she could saunter in confident in her beauty instead of feeling like an awkward little girl.

Taking a deep breath, she stepped inside Tom's room and stopped. He looked bad. His face, puffed in black and blue, looked like someone had beaten him with a baseball bat. His arm in a sling, a cast running from his wrist to his elbow, covered his fractured forearm. His right leg was immobilized with a brace. The guy was a mess. Alyssa took his good arm to check his vitals.

His eyes fluttered open, and he surveyed her with a hollow vacancy until recognition sparked in his gaze. "Alyssa?"

"In the flesh."

He swallowed, and his face contorted in

pain. "You look great. You're here?"

"I work here and have relatives in the area. Remember?"

He hesitated, attempted to blink. "Yeah, that's right." His eyes closed. "I can't believe you're here."

"They brought you in on Life Flight. What happened?"

"I tried to save her."

She poured a cup of water and brought a straw to his lips. "Save who?"

He sipped, and half of the moisture rolled out of the right side of his mouth. "Emily Kingston."

Alyssa cleaned his chin. "The movie star? How would you know her?"

His semi-lucid gaze settled on her face. "I'm a photographer."

"What happened to journalism?"

Besides pain, something flickered in his eyes. "That door closed. Life got in the way."

"But you always wanted to be a writer."

He groaned. His bloodshot eyes closed for a moment, then reopened. "Somebody attacked Emily, and I tried to rescue her. I didn't do anything wrong."

A sick feeling washed over Alyssa. Why would he even say that? She'd heard that line way too many times from Tom. Why had she forgotten the numerous hollow excuses he had given her during their time together?

His swollen hand covered hers. "I've missed

you."

Her heart flung itself like a canary trapped in her rib cage. Old emotions making her woozy; she snatched her hand back and gripped his bed railing.

Tom's eyes surveyed her, and a lopsided grin tried to form within the puffiness. "You still care." His voice merely a deep whisper. That same voice that promised so many things.

"Yes, I care. Actually, I still hurt. You took part of me and left me with nothing but a broken heart."

Tom squeezed her fingers. "Oh, Babe, I'm sorry. I loved you, I just wasn't ready to settle down, and all I could think of to do was run. You deserved better. I'm sorry." His eyes looked sincere, but how could she be sure with all the swelling? "I'm not the same guy I was. I've changed."

A knock on the door startled her. She stepped away from his bed.

A man with dark hair, wearing black slacks, a white shirt, and a dark tie stepped into the room. "Mr. Chambers, I'm Detective Truman." He pointed to his badge clipped on his belt. "I need to ask you a few questions."

Tom groaned as he maneuvered to raise up. "Sure."

Alyssa pushed the bed controls to lift his back and head.

The officer stepped closer. "I'd like to talk with you about Emily Kingston."

Tom swallowed and coughed. "Did you find her?"

"We were hoping you would tell us."

Alyssa started toward the door.

"Alyssa." Tom's voice halted her progress. "Wait, don't go."

She moved to the corner and busied herself looking at information on the computer.

Tom addressed the officer. "I talked to that other policeman."

For only a nanosecond, Detective Truman's face registered surprise, then resumed a placid expression. "Another policeman?"

"Yeah, he asked some questions."

The detective made a note. "Did you get his name? Could you describe him for me?"

"I couldn't focus very well. But he was a big guy, dark hair, muscular."

The officer looked at Alyssa. "Did you see anyone?"

"No, I'm sorry." Alyssa tried to think when someone else could have been in the room and made a mental note to discuss with Carla if she'd seen anyone.

The detective wrote something on his notepad, then turned back to Tom. "How about you tell me what happened?"

Tom groaned and went into a coughing fit.

Alyssa filled his cup with water and brought a straw to his lips.

He drank, then his semi-glazed gaze settled on the detective. "Emily's gate was locked. I rammed the car through, tried to get there. He was strangling her."

The detective's notetaking paused. "Who was strangling her?"

"I couldn't make out his face. Tall guy. He had his hands at her throat."

"Were you in the room?"

"No, on the hill."

"Why were you on the hill?"

"I'm a photographer."

"You were taking photos of Emily in the middle of the night?" The detective's voice took a hard edge.

"No." Tom's voice grew more assertive. "It wasn't that late. Check the camera's memory card; you'll see her attacker. I was hired to take photos of her."

"Who hired you?"

"Mirage Agency in Hollywood."

"Mirage?"

Tom blinked a few times as though processing. "I get paid by lots of different people for my work. I have the invoice back home. I can send it to you when I'm released."

The detective surveyed him for a moment. "So, you decided to photograph Emily at night?"

"I was told to take the pictures then." Tom grimaced and glanced at Alyssa.

"By *Mirage* Agency?" The detective's voice held disdain.

Tom hesitated a moment. "Yes."

"Had you been in contact before with

Emily?"

"Yeah, I met her a couple of times in a coffee shop. She wanted to thank me, said she appreciated how I took care only to publish the good shots of her. She was genuinely interested in my work." Tom glanced at the detective, then at Alyssa, and back to the officer. "Look. I was paid to take those photos at that time, and I assumed Emily was aware of when they would be taken. I'm not the bad guy here. Check my camera, and you'll see who attacked her."

The officer took a step closer, his back rigid. "We found your camera with photos of Emily in her nightgown. There was no one in her house ... only a blood trail leading outside. The blood was Emilys."

An even more sickly pale washed over Tom's already pale face. "You didn't see anyone else in the photos? Some guy attacked her. He was there. I tried to save her. I took photos. You have to find the photos."

The detective's presence seemed to enlarge as he loomed over Tom's bed. "Or, maybe you had an accomplice. Want to tell me what *really* happened and what you've done to Ms. Kingston??"

"I didn't do anything wrong. I tried to save her. I'm going to be sick." Tom turned his head, aimed for the floor ... and missed.

The detective stepped back and waited as Alyssa cleaned up the mess.

"Do not leave town." He handed Tom his

business card. "I'll be in touch."

Groaning, Tom never looked up. "I'm not going anywhere."

The officer nodded toward Alyssa, then left.

Tom kept his eyes closed. "I photograph celebrities. Stars love me. I respect their space, always thank them for photos, and work with their publicists to make sure the photos are attractive. I'm really good. The agency paid me because they said they heard I did great work. I was hoping this would be my big break." His voice slurred. "I didn't expect this kind of break."

Watching as Tom drifted off to sleep, Alyssa's stomach churned as she stood next to his bed. Seeing him again dredged up every emotion in the book.

His explanation sounded somewhat plausible about Emily, but photographing Emily at night while in her nightgown? The thought of him doing something other than what he said made her sick.

What had Tom done, and could she, and the police, believe him?

Seven

Cold seemed to come from within and seeping through Alyssa's ski jacket. Not even the down lining could keep out the frigid feelings.

Ice formed a sheen on the tops of most of the river rocks, and icicles dangled from the cliff face. At least having Sean sitting next to her, his shoulder touching hers, brought some warmth.

"I see why you like coming out here. It's beautiful." Sean's voice sent little puffs of vapor into the air. He smiled as his gaze met hers.

"Being out here gives me time to think." She tugged her coat tighter around her, then zoomed her camera lens to a snow-covered boulder in the river. The rock looked like it wore a white dunce cap. She felt like she was wearing one right now.

Early morning sun lit the sky in melon and peach colors. She focused her camera upriver and spotted two kayakers. Trying to ignore the cold, she aimed her camera and took several photos. Why would anyone want to kayak in freezing temperatures?

The light played on the water tops, shimmering between the boulders. The kayakers passed by laughing and talking.

Alyssa's shutter clicked as her camera took moments of time and placed them on the memory card.

However, some captured memories were better left alone. Tom had been someone she loved. Now, did he seem interested in her because he needed her help, or was he interested in getting back together? If only the medical profession had a truth stethoscope, one that told you the thoughts and true feelings of a beating heart.

She'd sheltered herself the last several years so much she didn't have much of a life. Maybe she should consider dating again. *No pain, no gain.* Wait, perhaps she needed a better slogan.

Sean tossed a rock into the river. "You remember that time we laid on the grass watching the sky, and the shooting stars were all around?"

Alyssa smiled at the thought. The high school years seemed so long ago. "That night, I could've sworn I could have touched the sky."

"Maybe that's another reason I started flying. It's cool to pray at 25,000 feet."

She nudged him with her shoulder. "No fair getting closer to God."

Sean surveyed her for a moment. "What's been bothering you?"

Alyssa turned away and half-focused on the river. "Stuff."

"Must be some heavy stuff."

She sat thinking, wondering. Maybe a guy's

viewpoint would help give her clarity. "Sean, I don't know what to do about something."

"I'm all ears."

"You remember the guy I dated in college?"

Sean picked up a rock and threw it hard into the river. "Not personally, but I didn't like him. He left you with a broken heart."

She stared off in the distance as her chest wound reopened with abandon. "Tom's back in town and one of my patients."

"Someone beat him up for being a jerk?"

"He was in a car wreck."

"Oh, sorry. What's he doing here?"

"He was photographing Emily Kingston."

"The movie star? I didn't know she was in the area. She's been off the radar lately."

"Yeah, and now she's missing, and the police are asking Tom questions."

"I knew I didn't like the guy." Sean's back stiffened. "Maybe, it's best you keep your distance."

"Kind of hard since he's on my nursing roster. He'll move soon to rehab."

Sean stared at the river, paused, then turned his gaze on her. "Are you still interested in him?"

"No." She hoped her response was convincing.

He surveyed her for a moment. "Good. I don't want anyone to break your heart again."

Moisture built in her eyes, and she looked away. Why did caring for people come with so much risk and so much pain? She'd loved Tom, and when things ended, her mangled heart continued beating behind a wall of self-protection.

Her grandmother had told her the only safe place for a heart was to be tucked safely in God's heart. Alyssa sighed. How she wanted her heart to beat again, to feel safe. She'd spent far too many years agonizing about Tom and not living.

She didn't close her eyes, but she did pray. *God, I need heart protection. Open my eyes, show me the truth, and please show me what You want me to do.*

~~*~*

Sean looked toward the river, but out of the corner of his eyes, he could still watch Alyssa. She always joked he was the brave one, but she was the bravest. Her parents had been stern, unforgiving, expecting her to be the best, do her best, do whatever it took to look good to the outside world. When they were kids, they'd been playing in a streambed, and she had cut her foot on a broken bottle. Leaving a trail of blood behind her, he'd helped her get home. When they arrived at her house, her dad screamed at her, scolded her for getting hurt, and told her to stop crying. Sean gulped hard. He still remembered her face and the look of hurt in her eyes.

Although Alyssa had always been there for

his James Bond-type antics, he always wondered if her taking care of him, treating him with sympathy and love, was what she'd desired and wished she had in her own life. Had her childhood caused her to keep her emotions in check and her heart walled off?

They sat, not speaking, just being together in the comfortable silence. He would always be there for her; in whatever way she would let him.

Alyssa looked his way. "You, ready to go?"

Sean stood and held out his hand. Alyssa let him pull her to her feet. He didn't release her hand and stepped closer. "You know I'm always here if you need me."

She nodded and looked up into his eyes.

His gaze remained on her face for a moment, then moved to her lips. Before he did anything, he straightened and wrapped his arm around her shoulder. "Come on. Let's get you out of the cold."

~~*~*

Alyssa nestled under Sean's strong arm. If Tom wasn't in the picture, would she be looking differently at Sean? But did Sean still see her only as a good friend? If he saw her as more than a friend, would she wish their relationship would progress? If she was honest with herself – yes.

How could she still feel something for Tom

and yet have a warm feeling, something more than friendship, blooming in her heart for Sean?

They walked along in silence. Alyssa took a deep breath and sighed. She needed a vacation, somewhere warm and tropical. She'd rest in a hammock with the sounds of lazy waves lapping the shoreline and warm sun in her face. Perhaps she'd drink a large glass of sweet iced tea like her grandmother used to make.

"You're smiling? Sean's voice interrupted her thoughts. "What you thinking?"

"I was visualizing being on a beach in a hammock."

"Sounds great. Can I join you?"

Alyssa's cheeks warmed at the thought of him sitting next to her on the beach in the sunshine. "If you had a transporter, I'd say beam us up."

Sean chuckled. "You know I am a pilot?"

"Oh yeah, ... I uh, ... maybe someday, huh?" Whew, when did it get so hot? She quickened her pace.

Her foot clipped a rock. Ankle twisting, she flailed at the air to keep her footing.

Sean grabbed her by the waist and held her tight against him. "I've got you."

Alyssa drew in a breath and looked up at his handsome face. Seriously handsome face. They had been friends forever, and now in his arms, he wasn't just a little neighborhood kid anymore; he was a man. A mighty fine man. He even smelled good. Alyssa laid her head against his chest.

She had two choices, laugh it off and see it as just a close friendship, or dive into something more. Hadn't she just prayed about what to do with her heart?

He rubbed her back. "Are you going to be okay?"

"Yes, but if you keep that up, I might drool."

He chuckled and kept rubbing. "All those times you took care of me, maybe it's my turn."

She swallowed hard as moisture built in her eyes.

His hand gently lifted her head to look at him. "Mind if I kiss you?'

Her knees weakened. "Oh yes. I... I ... don't mind."

Their lips met. A soft moan escaped her throat. If she had realized how good he could kiss, she would have done this much sooner.

The movies talked about time standing still, and now she knew it was true. She could stay here forever.

Eight

Sean drove his rental car to the Boise airport then parked. After the kiss with Alyssa, he had felt lighter than air. However, the drive back to her townhouse, and the goodbye once they arrived, had been awkward. She had seemed pleased and very willing to be kissed, but after had seemed hesitant and conflicted.

He understood part of what was going on. Tom injured, and in her care at the hospital, was a problem. His injuries might be real, but would he use them to lure Alyssa back into a relationship?

Sean groaned. Although she always said things were fine when she'd dated Tom, the toll the relationship had taken on her had been obvious. Her confidence had been gone, her playful spirit withdrawn, and now Sean saw it happening again.

He kneaded the tight muscle in the back of his neck, knowing all too well the dangers of falling for those who seemed to need care. A few years ago, he'd fallen hard for a girl who he thought had been an angel but was a devil in disguise. She'd convinced him how much she needed him, how terrible her childhood had been, and how awful her family was to her.

He'd tried to be her savior, take care of her, and make everything right for her.

Later, he found out that everything she told him had been lies and half-truths, used to manipulate him and those around her to get what she wanted. Thankfully, his eyes had been opened, but still, his regrets piled high.

God helped him move forward, had forgiven him for his wrongdoings, even helped him forgive that girl, but that didn't mean his failures were removed from his memory. Now, he just hoped and prayed Alyssa would not go back to her past and return to Tom.

After making his way through the airport, Sean strapped next to his co-pilot, Mark, in a corporate jet at the Boise airport. Hopefully, this flight would be uneventful since they were delivering a group of businessmen back to Friedman Memorial Airport near Sun Valley.

Taking a deep breath, Sean blew it out. He needed to concentrate on his job. Besides doing something he loved, flying helped with his perspective to see things from above life's problems. Just like a plane doesn't have a rear-view mirror, he needed to remember to keep his eyes on what is ahead, not on what was behind.

"Did you get the email about the emergency flight tonight to Salt Lake?" Mark's voice brought Sean back to the present.

"Yep, if all goes well, we should be back in plenty of time, and I won't be over my allotted flying hours. Do you know who we are delivering to the medical center?"

"A little girl, only four, with some rare disease I can't even pronounce. I can't imagine what her parents are feeling."

Sean's heart dropped. "I can't either. It must be awful. Thanks for getting me involved with that organization. It's worth every bit of my time to volunteer." Since moving to Idaho, he'd joined the pilots who transported those needing medical help. He might not be a nurse like Alyssa, but he was grateful to help those who needed to be transported to medical care. He'd met great people along the way, and there were several he continued to stay in touch with and pray for.

"Do you have any flights upcoming for Mr. Smith?" Mark grinned and did the air quotes sign with his fingers when he said the man's alias.

"Yes, he's requested my services next week. Even with all his money, he's a nice guy." Sean still couldn't believe his luck, or maybe he should say the blessing of flying the man to his business meetings.

"I wish I'd gotten his assignment. Flying someone that rich and famous has to be pretty cool."

"It is. Some wealthy people are proud and arrogant, but he's different. He took me to dinner one time after flying him to Salt Lake. I found out he didn't come from money; instead, he worked his way through all kinds of jobs before he came to head his multi-million-dollar business."

"Maybe that's part of why he's a good guy."

"Yeah, but I think it's deeper. He said he lived by God's rule to treat others the way he would want to be treated."

"Boy, can you imagine how different the world would be if people would live that way?"

"Definitely would be a nicer place."

Tower approval given; Sean taxied the plane to the runway and took to the air. Maybe he needed to remember that rule even when dealing with Alyssa's old boyfriend. Sean grimaced. He'd be nice, but he would be praying God would open Alyssa's eyes to see the truth.

Nine

Tired from tossing and turning when she should have been sleeping and still confused about the sweet time with Sean, Alyssa arrived at work and rode the elevator to the hospital floor she'd been assigned for the night. Time with Sean by the river had been good; kissing him had been fantastic, but would pursuing a relationship with him even be possible?

They weren't the same kids they used to be. Sure, they'd stayed in touch over the years, but their lives had gone separate ways. Tom had wounded, shredded her heart, and torn it to pieces, but still, she could sense her heart peeking around her ribcage, trying to be brave and love again.

Whatever happened with Sean, she needed to keep her distance and stay away from Tom. Hopefully, she could get someone to cover for her on her shift. And, if necessary, she'd ask for a transfer to another department while he was at the hospital.

The elevator doors opened, and her heart rammed up her throat. In front of her stood Tom's mother.

"Alyssa!" Mrs. Chambers enveloped Alyssa

in a way-too-tight hug, then stepped back and took Alyssa's hands in hers. "Look at you. You look all grown up, and now you're a real nurse."

"Mrs. Chambers, I'm surprised to see you." Tom's mother looked the same. Expensive, designer clothes, hair immaculate, the woman oozed money and prestige.

Mrs. Chambers tilted her head and smiled her fake smile. "Jane. You know I prefer Jane. After all we've been through, you can call me by my first name."

All they'd been through. The statement ignited Alyssa's every insecurity. During her years dating Tom, his mother had been syrupy sweet to her face and then would stab her in the back with snide comments to Tom and other family members. Why, and *how* had she forgotten that horrible time?

Hoping someone would be requesting her presence, Alyssa glanced down the hall. "I need to get to my shift."

Mrs. Chambers grabbed Alyssa's arm and drug her toward Tom's room. "Tell me what you know about Tom's condition. The other nurses and doctors are vague. They say he will be fine, but I don't know if I believe them. I'm going to stay in town for as long as it takes to ensure he gets the care he needs. I know you will be glad to help."

Alyssa spotted Carla at the nurse's station and untangled herself from Tom's mother. "Mrs. Chambers, I need to get to my shift. If you go to

Tom's room, I'll make sure the supervisor on duty can answer any questions you may have." She nudged Tom's mother toward the open door of his room. "I'll check in on you later."

Practically running at warp speed, Alyssa hurried to Carla's side and kept her voice low. "Help me!"

Carla turned toward her. "What's going on. Are you okay?"

"No, not okay. Definitely not okay. Ex-boyfriend's scary mother here. You've got to put me on another floor today or cover for me in Tom's room. There's too much from the past and so much going on now. I need distance. I'll work for you extra days, extra months, extra years, just please help."

"My, my, my, you are in need of some intervention. I'll be glad to help, and I'll take you up on your offer for an extra day. My daughter-in-love and son are coming to town in two weeks with my new baby granddaughter, and I'd love a little extra time with them."

"It's a deal. Where can I hide?"

"If you'll cover your other rooms, I'll take care of the Chambers situation." Carla picked up a clipboard, walked to Tom's door, and gave her a thumbs-up before stepping inside.

Alyssa hurried to start her rounds. Having Tom in the building was bad enough, but his mother added to the drama.

Alyssa sighed. Why had she even thought for a moment getting back with Tom was a good idea? For the years they dated, his mother had made Alyssa miserable, and if she was honest with herself, the time with Tom hadn't left her with many positive memories.

She'd prayed God would show her the truth, and now things were so obvious she wondered if she'd been wearing blinders all those years with Tom. Why had she spent any time thinking he had been her one true love? The only true thing about their relationship was her heart had been broken and discarded.

She sent up a prayer of thanks to God for keeping her from a relationship with a man who used her and a family who didn't care for her.

After finishing with the patients on her wing, she checked the hall before dashing toward the nurse's station. Hopefully, she could end the day without another run-in with Mrs. Chambers.

Carla motioned her behind the partition at the nurse's station. "I can see why you've been hiding. Tom's mother is rather overpowering. The good news is, Tom will be transferred to another rehab building tomorrow morning."

Alyssa plopped in a chair. "I'm so grateful he will be moved soon."

"Me too. And by the way, Mrs. Chambers kept prying me for information about you. I deflected her questions with my questions about her and her family. She does enjoy talking about herself, so I think the only thing she knows about you is that you are a nurse, and you live in the area."

"Thank you for helping."

"Of course." Carla nodded. "I protect my friends, and I protect my employees. I'll cover for you until your shift ends and he is out of our building."

"Excuse me." The detective who questioned Tom walked around the corner. "I need to ask you some questions." He pointed to Alyssa. "Is there somewhere private we could talk?"

"Sure." Alyssa's legs seemed to go numb for a moment before she could stand. "How can I help?"

Carla motioned for the man to enter. "I'll step out and let you two have the area."

He waited until she walked away, then turned to Alyssa. "I understand you and Tom dated. I need you to tell me everything about him and his visit to Idaho."

"I'm sorry, I don't know anything. We dated, but that was years ago in college. I haven't heard from him or been in contact with him since then. The only way I even knew he was in the area was because he was brought to our hospital."

"Interesting." He made several notes, then surveyed her for a moment. "He didn't contact you before he came? No phone calls? Was he staying with you? Has your relationship hasn't been rekindled?"

"*No.* Definitely not. Why would you even think that?" She knew the answer before he said anything else. *Mrs. Chambers*. The woman haunted her during her college years, and now she was here to make her life miserable again.

"Detective, I don't know anything about Tom. I haven't been in contact with him since college. I didn't know he was coming to Idaho, and I didn't even know he had become a photographer. I don't want anything to do with him or his mother. Unless there is something about what happened to him since he was brought to the hospital, I need to get back to my patients."

"One more question." His dark eyes surveyed her. "Where were you on the night Emily was taken?"

Alyssa gulped, blinked. "Here. I was here. I work nights, and I was here. You can check."

"I'll do that." The officer handed her his card. "If you think of anything helpful, or if Tom says anything to help in this case, please call me. I'll be in touch."

After he left, Alyssa shook her head. Did he think she had been involved in what happened? Thankfully, she had been on duty the night Tom was brought into the hospital, and they hadn't been in touch. Even if they checked her phone records, they wouldn't find any calls. What if they thought she had a burner phone? What if the police believed her trips to the mountain were for more than photographing?

Panic rising, she tried to pull her thoughts from that direction and silently prayed. Or more like made desperate calls to God, screams, and pleading for divine help.

Alyssa took a long, slow breath, then released it. Right now, she needed to focus and make her rounds.

She hurried down the hall, opened the door to Mr. Jensen's room, and stepped inside. Thankfully, no ugly comment came from the bed.

Without flipping on the light, she stood by the man's bedside. His face actually looked peaceful. *Was he dead?* She leaned closer and made sure his chest was moving in and out.

On the nightstand next to his bed was an open Bible. Maybe Mr. Jensen wasn't a vampire after all, or perhaps one of the nurses brought it in for protection.

Even in the dim light, she could see the words of Jesus in Matthew 11:28 had been highlighted in the Bible, *"Come to Me, and I will give you rest...."*.

Alyssa let the words wash over her. How she needed rest. Even with her many failures, she knew God cared.

"What do you want?" The gruff voice startled her, and she jumped back from the bed.

Quickly regaining her composure, she moved closer. "Mr. Jensen, I was just checking on you."

"Checking on me? In the dark? It looks like you're hiding to me."

"I'm sorry. I needed a moment to think."

"Interesting." His eyes seemed to bore into her soul. "Want to tell me what's going on?"

"I don't think, as your nurse, that would be appropriate."

"Balderdash, woman. You've been nursing me for several days and seen me at my worst. I don't want a troubled nurse handling my case, so get off your chest whatever is bothering you."

"Old boyfriend troubles."

He blew out a breath. "Men can be idiots."

"Yes, sir."

"Woman can be pretty stupid too, you know."

"Yes, sir."

"So, what are you going to do about old boyfriend troubles?"

"Try to avoid him, but that's easier said than done since he's one of my patients," Alyssa said.

"Hmmm, he's probably not going to get the best care, is he?"

"No sir, I mean yes, he will get the best care. I took good care of him yesterday, and the supervisor took over today." Alyssa paused. "It's not just him; his mother is in town."

"Mothers of old boyfriends. Sounds like a situation that calls for a tranquilizer dart."

"Mr. Jensen, we don't do things like that."

"Well, probably should. Life would be easier on us all if we could tranquilize half of the population."

Alyssa coughed to hide her giggle. To change the subject, she pointed to the Bible on his nightstand. "Have you been reading?"

"That's not mine. My wife left it for me. She's been trying to get me converted for forty years." His voice softened. "She's a good woman."

"A good wife is a good thing, and Christianity is pretty good too."

"I'll agree on the wife part, but I'm still contemplating the other."

"For forty years?"

He glared at her. "All *you* people have is a list of things not to do."

"Oh, Mr. Jensen, it's much more than that. Jesus Christ is the best thing. I need him every day to help me through every day."

He surveyed her for a moment. "Getting preachy there, nursey."

"I'm sorry, it just came out. I've really needed God so much these last few days. Not that I don't always need him, it's just that things are kinda crazy in my life right now." She glanced at Mr. Jensen, who was surveying her with a raised eyebrow and a studious gaze. "I'm sorry, I'll let you get some rest." Alyssa turned to go.

He reached for her. "Don't you need to take my blood pressure or poke me with something?"

"Well, while I'm here, I probably should record your vitals."

"Yes, you probably should."

Alyssa took his arm in her hands and took his blood pressure.

Mr. Jensen pointed to the Bible. "Let me tell you something. I've worked hard all my life, I've tried to be a good person, I've tried to be a good husband and father, and still, my wife says I've missed the main thing."

"Finding Christ is the best and main thing."

He didn't say anything for a long time, then patted her hand. "Thank you for talking to me." He smiled and closed his eyes. "Goodbye, Alyssa."

"See you around, Mr. Jensen." She closed his door and stepped into the hall.

"What on earth?" Carla grabbed Alyssa by the arm and hurried her to the nurse's station. "You are smiling after leaving Mr. Jensen's room? What is going on?"

"I had a good conversation with him."

"Really? If you had a good conversation with that man, I must put you in for a service reward." Carla directed her to the nurse's station. "Unfortunately, the situation with Tom Chambers and his mother is not good. As soon as your shift is over, I think you need to run. His mom is scary. She acts nice, but I wouldn't turn my back on her."

"For years, I thought it was just me, and I was imagining things, or I did something wrong."

"I think the only thing you did wrong was dating that boy in the first place. I'll be glad when they move him to rehab. His mom has kept me jumping with all sorts of over-the-top requests for Tom's care and then trying to get information about you."

"I'm sorry. Thank you for covering for me."

"No worries. Make another pass with the other patients and get out before the sun comes up. I'll be glad for us both when this shift is over."

After making her last round, Alyssa said goodbye to Carla and stepped back into the hallway.

"There you are!" Mrs. Chambers grabbed Alyssa by the arm and pushed her toward Tom's room. "I've been wondering what happened to you. You need to get in here right now. That policeman has been talking to my boy, and you need to help."

"Mrs. Chambers, I don't know anything that would be helpful."

"Well, that's a ridiculous statement. After all you have meant to Tom and our family, you need to hear what Tom says, and then you need to fix this."

As Alyssa was pushed into Tom's room, she sure wished she had that tranquilizer dart Mr. Jensen had suggested.

Tom gave her what seemed an apologetic smile from his still swollen face. "Sorry if Mother is coming on too strong. It's been kind of disturbing with all the police questions." He struggled to adjust himself.

"I guess so."

"That horrid policeman is accusing my boy of who knows what." Mrs. Chambers fluffed

Tom's pillow behind his head. "Tell her what you told me about Emily's boyfriend stalking her. If anything happened to that girl, it was his fault, not Tom's."

"That's right. I didn't do anything. Emily said she was scared of her boyfriend."

"He told the police." Mrs. Chambers interjected. "But that detective just kept asking questions like he didn't believe Tom. He even said Emily's boyfriend has an alibi because he had flown on a private plane to California. I don't believe him. Just because a plane left with someone, that doesn't mean it was her boyfriend."

Alyssa directed her attention to Tom. "The police are probably just being careful to question anyone involved. I'm sure they'll discover the truth soon."

Mrs. Chambers took a step closer and glared at her. "To find the truth, they need to be out there looking at other people and not bothering my boy. He is the one who tried to rescue her."

Alyssa stepped away and moved to the door. "Tom, I hope you feel better soon."

"Thanks. See you soon?"

"You'll be transferred to rehab, so I'm not sure."

His mother followed her. "Can we talk for a few minutes?" She smiled and turned back to Tom. "We'll be right back, sweetie."

Closing the door behind her, smile now gone, Mrs. Chambers faced Alyssa. "I heard you talking to a man about Christianity. I want you to stay away from Tom, but if you don't help my son in this mess with Emily Kingston, I'll report you for trying to ram religion down a helpless patient's throat."

Ten

Cold inside and out, Alyssa sat on a boulder by the river. The threat made by Tom's mother left her downright nervous. Since Tom's father was physically a large man and a prominent newspaperman, anyone who got on that family's bad side could face very negative repercussions.

How was she supposed to navigate through this mess? Even when Tom was moved to rehab, he probably wouldn't be able to leave town because of the police investigation.

Maybe she should take a vacation and see if Sean could fly her somewhere far away from the Chambers family. She stared at the sky. Running away wouldn't solve anything because there was no telling what Mrs. Chambers would do.

Alyssa rubbed her eyes, trying to stop the moisture building as a painful memory tumbled forward. During summer break from college, Tom had invited her to stay with him at his parent's house. Alyssa had arrived but didn't see Tom's car. Sitting outside, she texted Tom she was out front waiting. He had quickly replied he was running late but would be there soon.

Since it was night, Alyssa could see Mrs. Chambers inside the house, sitting at a desk in the study on her computer.

Alyssa watched as the woman answered her cell phone, then she rose to her feet and looked outside. Turning, the woman then shut off the light in the room. A few minutes later, the front porch light, along with all the lights in the house, went dark.

Alyssa shivered. Why hadn't she just driven away? Why had she stayed with Tom even though she knew she wasn't welcome? Why had she ignored the extremely obvious slight? Instead, when Tom finally arrived, she had gone inside and pretended everything was fine.

She'd dealt with insecurity all her life, thinking she wasn't good enough, pretty enough, or intelligent enough. She'd been determined to make Mrs. Chambers like and accept her, but it had only been a waste of time.

Alyssa wrapped her arms around herself. When she was younger, she'd believed if you were nice, people would be nice back to you. But that wasn't true. She'd tried to please people, but that never worked. She'd tried to please Tom and gotten in a relationship she shouldn't have, done things she regretted, and stayed with him because she had regretted the things she'd done.

She'd always felt a little insecure around Tom, wondered what he was doing when he was late or didn't call. She'd see him around campus hugging other girls, his phone ringing at odd times, and he wouldn't answer.

Another memory sprang to mind of a weekend where Tom said he was going away with his college roommate, Brad. But that next day, Alyssa had seen Brad on campus without Tom. She never found out where Tom really went or what he did. And when he returned, he kept talking about the great time he'd had with Brad.

Why had she stayed with Tom? She'd been so desperate to be accepted, to be loved. As a little girl, she'd been the skinniest, shortest, and wore glasses with the thickness of coke bottles. By the time she reached college, friends told her she was cute; then, when Tom came along and said she was beautiful, she'd clung to him, desperate for reassurance.

Alyssa took her camera in her hands and looked through the viewfinder but couldn't see anything. Shaking her head, she removed the lens cap. Now, she could see, zoom in, and focus.

Maybe God was finally removing what blocked her memories. Everything was coming so clear now, like the lens cap on her eyes had been removed.

She'd wasted her college years loving a man even though she'd wondered all along if he really loved her. She had hoped Tom would marry her so her guilt would go away about their relationship, that she would have some security and stability, but marriage to Tom wouldn't have fixed anything.

Insecurity had kept her from standing up for herself and not getting away from Tom and his family. How she longed to stop looking back at the past, but moving forward wouldn't be possible if she kept tripping over what was behind her.

After all these years, why did she still feel guilty and confused? God knew her many failures, knew all the things wrong she'd done, and she'd apologized to him a million times. Maybe not a million, but still, she couldn't get rid of the guilt feelings.

The water in the river flowed free and easy, sparkling in the sunshine, splashing and playing across rocks and boulders. That's what she wanted to do, what she wanted to be, moving free in God's forgiveness.

"God, open my eyes, show me how." She whispered. Looking up into the vast sky, she prayed, asking again for forgiveness, and asking that God would help her remember she was forgiven.

As she sat there thinking, she remembered the Bible promised God would wash away sins and no longer remember those sins.

God couldn't lie, so that meant the promises were true. Oh, how she wanted to live in the freedom of forgiveness. She needed to forgive herself, and when the memory of sin returned, she needed to remember it wouldn't be God reminding her.

Another verse came to mind about trusting

in the Lord. So, did that mean she was supposed to trust that God had forgiven her?

She took out her phone and brought up her Bible app to look up the verse and the different translations. One stood out...*Trust in the Lord completely, and do not rely on your own opinions. With all your heart rely on him to guide you, and he will lead you in every decision you make. Become intimate with him in whatever you do, and he will lead you wherever you go.*

Intimate with God, relying on him with all her heart. Yes, that's what she needed. If she could do that, if she *would* do that, it would be okay, and her heart would heal.

Alyssa took a few more photos, deleting those from her memory card that weren't the best. How she wished she could delete the years with Tom, erase and purge her past.

Maybe she could do a few things that would help. Photos were made to allow remembering, to capture memories to be viewed later. When she got home, she needed to purge the old pictures, the photo albums in her closet, and the digital photos on her computer. Remove ones that reminded her of the negative times, get rid of those that weren't the most photogenic, even delete the outdoor shots that weren't the best, and definitely get rid of any pictures that no longer made her smile. Why hold onto the documentation of sad memories?

The thought made her spirit jump, like

something good would come from all of this. Something new.

Rising to her feet, she walked to her car. It was time to move on. Buckling in, she started the journey home. She had some major cleaning to do. Hopefully, by the time her next shift started, Tom would be moved to rehab, and she wouldn't have to see him or his mother again.

Still, she was curious, what if Tom was right? What if what happened to him was all a setup, and he didn't have anything to do with Emily's disappearance? Then again, what if Tom was guilty?

The sound of a horn startled her.

A deer stood on the road in front of her, and in the oncoming lane, a truck barreled toward her.

Eleven

Adrenaline surging, Alyssa turned the wheel of her car, slammed on her brakes, and screeched to a stop on a small gravel road. The deer casually looked her way and trotted off.

Leaning back in her seat, she thanked God she didn't wreck.

In the distance, someone screamed. A slender woman with shoulder-length, silver hair came running toward her. "Help, help, help! My husband fell."

Alyssa hurried out of her car and followed the woman down the road. Outside a house, under a ladder, a grey-haired man lay sprawled on the ground. She knelt next to him to check for injuries.

"I was just about to call 911." The woman's frantic voice hovered above her. "But it takes them so long to get out here, and I was praying God would send someone to help."

The man groaned and gazed up at Alyssa. "I'm okay, just fell."

"Sir, please don't sit up. I'm a nurse. We need to take precautions. Take slow, easy breaths."

The woman gasped. "You're a nurse? Thank

God!"

Alyssa kept focused on the man. "Sir, are you able to move your feet and fingers?"

He complied with movement in his legs and hands. He struggled to sit up. "I'm sure I'm okay; I just got the wind knocked out of me."

"Take it slow, sir." She helped steady him as he rose to an upright position.

"I'm fine. I just slipped. It could happen to anyone."

The lady stroked his shoulder, then turned to Alyssa. "I told him to wait on the project until our son-in-law could help, but he wanted to do things himself. Anyone at the age of seventy-two should be a little more careful."

"Okay, you're right." He grinned at them both. "I should have waited. Lesson learned. Now, can I stand up?"

"If you promise to stay off the ladder." The lady interjected.

Grateful the man seemed fine; Alyssa helped him to his feet and looked at the woman. "Since there was a fall and he might have hit his head, I'd suggest keeping an eye on him for the next twenty-four hours."

The man brushed off his jeans. "I promise to stay off the ladder. And I'm sure she will watch me." He grinned and nodded toward his wife.

"I'll watch him a like a hawk. By the way, I'm Carrie, and he's Robert. We're the Wrights. Thank you so much for stopping to help."

"I'm Alyssa. I can't take credit for the stop. I

swerved to avoid a truck and a deer."

"I don't believe in accidents or chance. I was praying, and you came skidding into our driveway. I'm so grateful you stopped. Can we pay you for your services?"

"No, you don't need to do that. It's my pleasure to help."

"Could I at least make you some hot coffee, tea, or hot cocoa?"

"She does make the best hot chocolate in the world," Mr. Wright said. "She even won a contest a few years ago."

"Well, when you put it like that, I might take you up on that. I can't stay long; I work nights at the hospital and need to get home to catch some sleep."

Mr. Wright directed Alyssa to their front door. "Sleep catching is an art. Since my retirement, I've finally got that perfected. I take great pride in being able to nap during the day and still sleep through the night."

Mrs. Wright giggled. "He's proud of his achievements."

Feeling comfortable with the couple, Alyssa followed them into their home. The smell of something yummy along with a new house smell greeted her as she stepped into the house with a modern touch and clean lines. The simple but elegant furniture looked brand new. The back wall of the family room was lined with windows overlooking the river. What looked like family photos of children and grandchildren sat on the mantle of the stone fireplace.

"Your home is beautiful, and you have a gorgeous view out your windows."

"Thank you," Mrs. Wright said. "We just finished building a few weeks ago to be closer to family. Our daughter and her family just live up the road. They're on vacation this week, so Robert thought he would take care of a few things himself."

"I handled everything we needed just fine until the ladder incident." He took three mugs out of a cabinet in the kitchen then turned to Alyssa. "What would you like, coffee, tea, or some of my wife's famous hot cocoa?"

"I'd love to try the hot cocoa. Thank you."

"Would you like a biscuit? Carrie just made them this morning, and we have extra."

"Wow, you spoil me. Thank you."

Mrs. Wright opened her oven door and brought out a tray filled with her homemade goodies. "It's our pleasure. I am grateful God sent you to us."

Mr. Wright handed Alyssa a mug with steamy hot chocolate, a plate with two biscuits, and motioned her to the table. "You'll have to forgive Carrie. She taught young adults at our church for thirty years. I think she's having withdrawal since we moved up here to the mountains."

"Please don't apologize. I love God too."

"That's great. It looks like Carrie's prayer was answered in sweet ways."

Alyssa sat across from the couple and wrapped her hands around the warm cup.

"You mentioned you're a nurse," Mrs. Wright said. "So, what brings you out to the mountains early in the morning?"

"I like to come up here to take photos by the river. It's a great way to relax before going back home to catch some sleep before my next shift."

"Well, feel free to stop by our place anytime. Our family owns the property along the river for the next mile."

"Thank you. I work the night shift, so I'm usually pretty early. I wouldn't want to bother you."

"We get up before dawn, so come by anytime. Robert used to work long hours, and we just got in the habit. We both love early mornings when the world is quiet. Sometime I'll have to show you my favorite spot down the river; it's perfect for taking photos." Mrs. Wright pointed to a picture on the wall. "I took that one a few weeks ago."

Alyssa admired the beautifully framed photograph of the snowy river. "That's beautiful."

"It's not hard to get a wonderful photo of God's creation. He did the hard work; I just capture the beauty he created."

"You like to take photographs?"

"Yes, but I'm not a professional. I just love sitting by the river and spending time with God."

"You two sound like peas in a pod." Mr. Wright grinned at them both. "Carrie, give the girl your phone number so she can contact you next time she's up our way."

"I'd love that." Mrs. Wright gazed at Alyssa. "I mean, if you would like to."

"Yes, ma'am." Alyssa nodded. After they exchanged phone numbers, they continued to visit.

An hour later, Alyssa said goodbye to her new friends and headed home. How sweet that she had been praying for God's guidance, and she just happened to be the answer to someone else's prayer.

Maybe God was trying to show her to keep praying, move forward, and trust that he would direct her steps. Hopefully, those steps would lead to her favorite pilot.

Twelve

After a significant cleanup of her photos and the best night's sleep she'd had in weeks, Alyssa stepped out of the hospital elevator at work.

Carla waved from the nurse's station and motioned her over. "During the day, Tom's situation took a turn for the worse."

"Why, what happened?"

"He got violently ill. He's doing better, but he's probably going to be on our floor for a few more days. The day shift said Tom's mom was driving everyone crazy. I hope the woman is going to go back to her hotel. If not, it's going to be a long shift. But don't worry, Tania is helping out tonight.

Alyssa breathed a sigh of relief. Tania was a great nurse and could handle the most challenging patients.

"Plus, I assigned her to handle Tom and his parents." Carla continued.

"His parents? They are both are here?"

"Yes, and they are on the warpath. I'd suggest steering as clear as you can from Tom's room."

"You got it. Thanks for having Tania on the floor tonight."

"Did someone say my name?" Tania, her teal scrubs highlighting her beautiful brown skin, walked toward them.

"I'm so glad you are here." Alyssa hugged her friend.

"Uh, huh." Tania grinned and hugged her tight. "You're just grateful I'm running interference from your old boyfriend's family."

"I owe you. Name your price."

Tania smiled big and chuckled. "Let's have breakfast together one morning. There's a new place that just opened I've been dying to try."

"Sounds like a great plan."

"Alyssa!" Mrs. Chambers stormed their way. "I've been waiting for you."

Tania stood in front of Alyssa. "Mrs. Chambers, how can I help?"

"You can do your job and take care of Tom." She spit out the words with force and tried to side-step Tania. "I want to see Alyssa."

"Excuse me?" Carla, rising to her full six-foot towering height, stepped forward. "You do *not* talk to my nurses like that."

Mrs. Chambers took a step back and pasted on a smile that did not reach her eyes. "I'm so sorry." She dabbed at her dry eyes. "I've just been so worried about my boy." She covered her face as though overcome with emotion. "Please forgive me." The lady's melodramatics were worthy of an Oscar.

Carla and Tania surrounded the woman and directed her back to Tom's room.

Mrs. Chambers glanced over her shoulder, her dry eyes lasering Alyssa with malice, then she feigned she was crying as she stumbled against Carla as though too weak to continue.

Alyssa turned away, prayed like crazy, wheeled her computer cart in front of her, and hurried to check the other patients.

How was she supposed to get through the next few nights and avoid Mrs. Chambers? The verse came to mind about trusting in God. She sighed. Trusting God when everything was going well was sure easier than on days like these. However, wasn't that what trust was all about; trusting God in good and bad times? Some days that seemed so very hard.

She stopped outside Mr. Jensen's room. Surprised he was still on their floor; she opened the door. Without turning on the light, she peeked to see if he was awake.

"Yes, I'm still here." He grumbled. "Go ahead and turn on those mega-beams from the ceiling."

She switched on the light and checked his latest information on the computer.

He let out a guttural growl. "The doctor didn't release me because my blood pressure was too high. Maybe that's normal; how do doctors know what's normal? We are all different people. I think I was born with high blood pressure."

"Well, based on your records, yesterday, you were heading into the stratosphere."

"If you want my blood pressure to drop, get me out of here."

She checked his vitals. "I'm sorry, your numbers are going down, but they are still high. Hopefully, the new medication will work soon."

"Yeah, right. Throw more drugs at the old guy. Have you heard all the side effects there are with medications? The commercials have all those happy, smiling, healthy-looking people doing all sorts of happy, healthy things while the voice in the background lists the three thousand things that could happen, all of which usually ends in death."

She tried not to giggle. "Maybe if you wouldn't think about stuff like that, your blood pressure would go down."

"I just want to go home." His voice sounded like a little boy.

"Mr. Jensen, I'm so sorry. Get some sleep; tomorrow will be better."

He shook his head, his eyes pleading. "Tell me something good, Alyssa."

"Well, from the records, you're healing nicely from your surgery."

"No, I mean tell me something good about life. I'm sick of the news only reporting tragedies, sickness, politics, and negativity."

"I guess we could all use a little good news. So, let's see. God loves us." She paused and grinned his way. "He loves you. There are still good people in the world. There are people who want to make this world a better place by doing good things. There are moms and dads who love their kids. There are rescued kitties and puppies given to good homes. And, you told me the other day you have a good wife."

"Yes, I do. I'm ready to get home."

"I know it's hard to be separated from those you love." She glanced next to his bed at the Bible, now sitting open in a different place. "Have you been reading?"

"Yes." Mr. Jensen's gaze met hers, a tiny spark now showing in his gaze. "John 3:16 is more than a sign held up at sports events."

"Definitely." Regardless of who might be listening, she wasn't going to miss her chance. "It's the best news there is."

"Yes, it is. I know that now." He smiled, sighed, and laid back down. After a few deep breaths, he looked her way. "Maybe if you retook my blood pressure, you might get a different reading."

She complied and grinned at the results. "Well, look at you, Mr. Jensen. Your blood pressure is perfect."

"Make sure you make a note of that. I need to get home and take my long-suffering wife on a much-needed vacation and let her know her husband is a new man."

"I'll make sure to note your great blood pressure in your records. And what else you shared is the best news I've heard in a long time."

"Thank you for all you did for me while I

was here." He smiled and closed his eyes. "I'm grateful our paths crossed."

Alyssa wheeled her cart to the door, turned off Mr. Jensen's light, then checked to make sure the coast was clear. Fortunately, the hall was quiet. She smiled to herself, thinking what she would have missed if she hadn't come in tonight.

She continued to make her rounds then dropped back by the nurse's station.

Carla looked up from her computer. "Hey, how are things?"

"Good. Everyone seems to be doing pretty well for the shape they are in, and Mr. Jensen's blood pressure is back to normal. He's hoping he'll get home tomorrow."

"That is good news. You've been good for that man."

"I'm going to miss him."

Carla stopped typing on the computer and gazed at Alyssa like she had grown two heads. "Well, if you can survive Mr. Jensen, it's probably time to visit your old boyfriend. Tom is stable and doing better. His parents stepped out for the rest of the night. He asked for you a little while ago. Do you want to go see him?"

Alyssa drew in a long breath and blew it out. "Maybe I should. You sure his parents aren't coming back anytime soon?"

"I don't think they'll return before the morning. They gave me their number at the hotel where they're staying to give to the next shift."

"Okay, better make the most of the opportunity." She voiced a silent prayer and made her way to Tom's room. Opening the door, she stepped inside and tiptoed to his bedside. The gash on his face continued to show signs of healing, and the color on his skin did look more normal. His handsome features had returned.

"Hey." He struggled to shift his body. "I thought you were avoiding me."

"Maybe a little, but I was avoiding your mom. She's been pretty intense."

"Yeah, she's not made things easier for me and definitely not easy for you. Alyssa, I know I hurt you in college, and I'm sorry. But I didn't hurt Emily Kingston."

Although she appreciated the somewhat apology, it was too little too late. "Have you heard anything else on the investigation?"

"Just more stuff that makes me look like the bad guy. If I could get out of here, I'd drive up and check around her cabin. Maybe the police missed something."

"I don't think that would be a good idea. The last thing you need to do is go where they're investigating a crime."

Tom raked his hand through his hair. "I'm being framed, and I can't do a thing about it. Is there anything you can do to help? Anybody you can talk to for me?"

"I don't know anyone. I'm sorry. I'll pray for

you."

He groaned. "Yeah, right, you do that. Lots of people say that, but they don't do anything. They flip up a supposed prayer and then go along their merry way."

"I promise to pray, and I'll try and think of something I can do or ask around if anyone knows someone."

"Thanks. My father is also looking into what he can find out. Would you mind if I got your phone number? Or, at least let me give you mine. I really need help."

She hesitated. "How about you give me your number, and I promise to call if I find out anything. And, please ask your mom not to attack me?"

"It's a deal." Tom reached for her. "I'm sorry I hurt you. I was an idiot to let you go."

She stepped back. "Yes, you were."

Thirteen

Back home, Alyssa sat at the kitchen table and, using her laptop, scoured online news reports about Emily Kingston's disappearance. Fortunately, Tom's name wasn't mentioned, only that the police were questioning a person of interest.

The more she thought about it, the more she researched, the more she believed Tom was being framed. But why?

Tom mentioned Emily's boyfriend, David, had an alibi. The police said he was listed on the manifest on a plane, but could David have had someone else pretend to be him and fly under his name?

Alyssa speed-dialed Sean's number and left him a message. Maybe he would have some ideas and could help answer some questions.

"What you doing?" Kat's voice came from over her shoulder.

Alyssa pointed to her notes. "I'm thinking Tom is innocent and being framed for Emily's disappearance."

Kat took a breakfast bar from the cabinet. "So, you've gone from wanting to beat old boyfriend to rescue old boyfriend?"

"I guess so. When you look at the facts, I don't understand why the police keep questioning Tom. Then again, he was on a hill photographing her at night."

"That is creepy." Kat wrinkled her nose. "Was he stalking her?"

"I guess that's what the police think. But if Tom was guilty, why would he ram the gate? The detective mentioned there was a blood trail that was Emily's blood, but where did the trail lead? If Tom had been found unconscious, he couldn't have been the one who attacked her. And if Tom was passed out, who called for Life Flight? So, why then did that detective keep questioning him?"

"Interesting points. But why was he photographing her at night? The creep factor is big on that one. Why would he ram her gate? Was he ramming it to attack her? Or did he attack Emily and then come back and ram the gate to pretend he was innocent? Why is there Emily's blood, and no one knows where Emily is now? Tom was found at the scene of the crime, so I'd be questioning him too."

"But if he was going to attack her, he couldn't have been successful if he was injured in a car accident. I don't believe he would have injured himself. Somebody else had to be involved."

"Okay, but who?" Kat made her a cup of coffee using their single-serve machine and sat beside her.

"The detective even questioned me."

"*What?* Why would he do that?"

"I guess since Tom and I used to date and since I live here, maybe the police thought I might be involved."

"Ouch. That's not good. You were at work that night, though. You have an alibi."

"Yes, and I'm grateful I do. Okay, let me think. Emily's an actress; maybe it's a crazed fan or an evil plot to frame Tom. But why would someone want to frame him if he's just a photographer?"

"I know. It doesn't make sense." Kat munched on her breakfast bar for a moment. "Well, it could if you're an actress wanting publicity."

"A publicity stunt?"

"It's not like that sort of thing doesn't happen all the time."

"Maybe, but what if Emily was attacked and abducted by some evil person, and Tom was the only witness? Maybe a crazed fan grabbed her and made a run for it."

"If that's what's going on, then Tom would be in danger. Whoever attacked Emily would probably attack him to keep him quiet."

"Yikes, that's right." Alyssa sat back in her chair. "The other day, Tom got violently ill. I wonder if there is more than what we thought."

"Maybe someone tried to poison him?"

"Surely not. Maybe we're thinking too much on the dark side."

"Or maybe you're not getting dark enough. We live in evil times."

"That's a disturbing thought." Alyssa rubbed the goosebumps forming on her arm.

"Yes, but it's true. Then again, this week, we are working on writing dark poetry. Here's my latest." Kat stood. "Life is hard, evil, and dark. In this shadowy world, we must make our mark. Be aware, be brave, be bold, don't let this world turn you cold. Be a light, keep shining bright, fly above like a kite, no matter how this world bites."

Alyssa coughed to keep from laughing. "That's great."

Kat nudged her. "No, it's not. It's corny, but the guys will love it."

"It must be nice to have an adoring audience."

"Yes, it is. You need to come with me sometime. The guys would love you too. Next week we will be working on our Pieku's."

"Don't you mean Haiku? Where you have to have three lines, the first and third line is five syllables, and the second line is seven syllables? I don't know why I know that. I guess because it's such a strange form of poetry."

"Yeah, that's it. It's not too hard. But our Haiku is a Pieku. Whoever writes the best Haiku about a pie wins a pie, therefore it's a Pieku contest. Here's the one I'm working on. The apple delight... In buttery golden crust... Beckons to my waiting mouth."

"Okay... I hope you win a buttery golden crust apple pie and bring it back to the house."

"Me too. Either way, it will be fun." Kat put on her jacket and walked to the door. "I better get to work. Have a great day sleeping and whatever else you do before your night shift."

Alyssa said goodbye to her friend then turned back to taking further notes about Tom's situation.

Several minutes later, the doorbell interrupted her thoughts. Did Kat forget her keys? Alyssa hurried down the hall and peeked through the peephole.

Sean, grinning from ear to ear, stood on her front stoop. Good thing she still had on her scrubs from work.

Alyssa opened to let him enter. "Well, hey. What are you doing here?"

"You left a message for help" His eyes sparkling, he leaned toward her. "so here I am."

Heat rose to her cheeks. He was so handsome, so thoughtful, and so kind. Her heart peeked around her ribcage and tiptoed forward.

She gulped to find her voice. "You didn't need to come over."

"I know, but while I'm still in the area, it was a great excuse to see you again."

A little wobbly in the knees, she led him to the table. "I'm glad you're here. Can I get you some coffee?" When he shook his head no, she sat down next to him.

"What you doing?" He pointed to her laptop

and notes.

She hesitated a moment. She'd rather talk about Sean and spend time with him, but maybe he could answer some questions. "I think Tom has been framed, and the more I look into things, the creepier things are becoming."

"I've read a few articles online about her disappearance. Not much to go on as of yet. Is Tom their person of interest?"

"Probably. Let me ask you a question. If someone flies on a private plane, is there a way to make sure it was the person listed on the manifest? Could someone pretend to be that person?"

"Pilots are careful to check identification, but I guess anything is possible."

"Since you fly and are a pilot, and you probably know other pilots, would you maybe want to do a little detective work for me?"

Sean's gaze met hers, and he was quiet a moment. "I will do that for you, but not for Tom. You sure you're not interested in him?"

Was she still interested in Tom? No, it was over. Alyssa looked into Sean's eyes, those kind eyes that had been with her throughout the years. The past was past, and it was time to jump forward. "I am a hundred percent sure. To be honest, I've kind of got my eye on someone else." She grinned as heat flamed her cheeks. "Someone I've known for a long, long time." She held out her hand toward Sean.

"Really?" His fingers entwined with hers, his

gaze searching her face. He leaned closer and kissed her. "I've been waiting a long time to hear you say that."

"We've been friends forever. Do you think it's going to be weird dating? Plus, I'm two years older than you, I work nights, and you work in another town."

"We can sit here and analyze, or we can just see what happens. Age doesn't matter; we're both adults. I sometimes fly during the day, sometimes at night. I work in another town, but I'm a pilot, so I think we'll be just fine."

"Okay, but what do you think our families would say?"

"Alyssa, our families have known each other for years. They'll be fine. I think we should just skip the dating and go right to marriage."

"*What?*" As horrified as her voice sounded, part of her would eagerly jump in his arms.

"Just kidding. Somewhat." Sean wiggled his eyebrows. "Can we just enjoy being together without overthinking?"

"Yes, I'm sorry. It feels like a big step but not a big step." Alyssa paused and looked into his tender eyes. "I'm comfortable with you."

He grinned. "So, let's just continue being comfortable friends. I'm not asking you to jump in bed with me, although the thought does cross my mind." His face flamed red, and he cleared his throat. "Sorry, just being honest here. But I do want to date you in a way that honors you as a lady and honors God.

"That sounds nice."

"Yes, it does. Alyssa, I've made some pretty serious mistakes over the years, and I want to do things the right way now. It's not going to be easy, which is probably why I live in another town." He pushed out of his chair and stood. "I better be going."

"But you've only been here a few minutes."

"If I stay much longer, I may not be quite the gentleman I want to be." Sean kissed the top of her head. "I love you, Alyssa. I always have, and I always will."

Her heart jumped, twirled in her chest, leaned back, and sighed. Before she passed out from joy, she grabbed his hand and stood to her feet.

Alyssa kissed him. "I love you too."

Sean held her close for what seemed to be hours. With a slight groan, he stepped back. "I better go. I don't want to, but I better."

She giggled and walked him to the front hallway.

He opened the door, then turned toward her. "I won't be able to see you for a few weeks. I've got some things to take care of back home and then am booked to captain several flights."

Alyssa smiled. "You know where to find me."

Sean leaned toward her. "You know, you could just fly away with me."

She laughed and pushed him out the door. "You have got to go before I run off with you.

We shouldn't rush and do anything rash."

"Right." Sean took her arm and pulled her gently against his chest. "Even though we've known one another forever, we wouldn't want to be rash or rush."

"Smarty-pants." Breathing in his clean scent, listening to his heartbeat, Alyssa nestled in his embrace. "Well, I don't want you to rush right now. This is nice." She stayed in his arms until the cold caused her to shiver. "I better let you go."

"Nope. Not going to happen. Now that I've got you, I won't let go. So, I will be back." He kissed her and ran to his car. "I love you!"

"I love you too." She closed and leaned back against the door. Did she just tell Sean she loved him? Really say it, out in the open, like it was true, and right, and wonderful? *Yes!*

Floating to the kitchen, she grabbed a bite to eat, then went to her room, curled up in bed, and glided into a deep sleep.

When her alarm went off, she took a shower, ate a quick bite, and drove to the hospital. Her feet still barely touched the floor as she walked to the nurse's station to start her night shift.

"We need to talk." Carla stood and faced her. "Tom's been moved to a rehab facility, and this morning, Mrs. Chambers filed a formal complaint with the hospital against you."

Fourteen

"What?" Room spinning, Alyssa grabbed hold of the counter. "What did she say I did?"

"Mrs. Chambers accused you of being derelict in your duties and harassing a helpless patient to become a Christian."

"What? Derelict in my duties? You know that's not true. As for the helpless patient. I did talk to Mr. Jensen, but I didn't harass him in any way."

Carla surveyed her. "I know this complaint has nothing to do with you and everything to do with Mrs. Chambers. Fortunately, since I'm your supervisor, the complaint came directly to me. Unfortunately, we will have to go through the formal hospital process. There will be an investigation."

"Oh, Carla." Alyssa collapsed into a chair. "This makes me so sad, angry, hurt, and frustrated. If she wanted me to help Tom, this sure wasn't the way to go about it. She's always had it out for me."

"It's a distraction none of us need. We'll work this out and make sure it doesn't cause you any difficulties further down the road."

"Hey." Tania hurried toward them. "Carla,

let me know. I came as fast as I could." She knelt by Alyssa and hugged her. "You don't worry. We're going to help you get through this."

"Thank you." Alyssa glanced at her friends. "Thank you both. What do I do right now?"

"Today, go about your regular schedule," Carla said. "I'll get my end of the paperwork completed, and before you leave in the morning, we can sit down together and work through what else needs to be done. Since Mrs. Chambers has dealt with numerous nurses, there hasn't been one who has had anything nice to say about her. We know this complaint is about her being a vindictive woman. Still, we've got to go by the book. I've talked with Human Resources, and our HR guy is one of the best. He's promised to make sure everything is handled fairly and make certain you and the hospital are covered."

"I've been thinking," Tania said. "Mrs. Chambers told you she wanted you to help Tom, but then she filed a complaint against you. I think she wants to make sure you don't get back with her son."

"I agree. She never liked me." A disturbing thought came to mind. "Wait a minute; I just remembered Mrs. Chambers had come to visit Tom right before graduation. He avoided me after that. I always thought it was something I did or said that drove Tom away. Maybe his mom was behind what happened to us?"

Tania crossed her arms and nodded.

"Sounds like that woman has some major issues. I'll file paperwork of my own to help in your case."

Alyssa tried to shut off her thoughts as she worked her shift. She'd gone from walking on air about Sean to being slammed to the ground by a wicked woman. How she wished people would understand how much words hurt. Unfortunately, some people's normal mode of communication were lies, and they only used their words as weapons and for manipulation.

Once her shift was over, the meetings with the HR guy complete, and the first round of paperwork done, Alyssa stopped by the cafeteria to get a cup of coffee.

Victoria waved her over. "Well, howdy, friend. I've missed you."

"Sorry I haven't stopped by lately. Lots going on."

"What's wrong?"

"Life is a mess right now. Old boyfriend problem and old boyfriend's mother filed a formal complaint against me."

"Oh, dear. That's terrible about the complaint. Is he the one that left your heart broken?"

"One and the same. He's here in the hospital, and his mother is making my life miserable."

"I am so sorry." Victoria glanced around and motioned her to a table. "It's quiet right now. Sit down, and I'll get you a cup of coffee with extra whip cream."

Alyssa sat and rested her head in her hands. Even though things looked hopeful about resolving the complaint made by Mrs. Chambers, the investigation could drag on for who knew how long. She should never have dated Tom, gotten in a relationship with Tom, or had anything to do with Tom or his family. Why did they have to be here now, and why this latest attack by Mrs. Chambers?

Concern etching her face, Victoria handed Alyssa a large coffee and sat across from her. "Is there anything I can do to help?"

"I wish. People can be so mean. Why can't life be easier? Why do some people have to make other people miserable?"

Victoria shrugged and shook her head. "I sure wish I could answer those questions for you and all of us."

Alyssa felt like pounding the table. "I want to do something, fix something, correct things."

"Ah, the nurse in you wants everything healed."

"Yes, I do. Fix the past, fix the present, and fix everyone to be nice to one another," Alyssa said.

"I'll vote for that. That would be nice for all of us."

"I know I'm supposed to trust God, but trusting God is so blasted hard in real life, especially when things are tough."

"I understand. It's not easy. One thing that

helps me is when I stop and think about a bird with outstretched wings, flying in the sky, gliding, and soaring on air currents. Suffering, trials, and hardship exist, but by trusting God we fly on God's wings above the problems. Trust gives us wings."

"That sounds nice, but I feel like a bird that keeps trying to fly, and then life comes and bashes me to the ground." Alyssa flicked away the tear that ran down her cheek. How she wished she had wings to fly above this mess.

Victoria laid her hand on Alyssa's arm. "I think we all feel like that sometimes. We're all going to struggle. It doesn't mean we have to be perfect because we have a perfect Savior. Alyssa, God cares, and he will help you through whatever you are going through."

"I hope so." Alyssa rubbed at her eyes. "Right now, I'm just tired. I'm sorry I'm not handling things better. My life isn't bad; I even have some good things happening; it's just that the hard stuff is hard."

"Give yourself some slack, or better yet, give yourself grace. Go home and get a good day's rest. You're going to get through this. If I can help in any way, let me know. I'm so sorry, but work calls." Victoria excused herself and hurried back to her station as several customers walked in the door.

Alyssa finished her coffee and waved goodbye to her friend. Even though she was tired and frustrated, she did have many things to be grateful for. She had Sean, a good job, a good roommate, and good friends.

Thankfully, no matter what happened, Mrs. Chambers would only be a blip on the radar screen of eternity. She just hoped the woman would only be a small blip that disappeared soon.

Fifteen

Standing in front of the pilot, Sean held up his phone with a photo he had downloaded of Emily's boyfriend, David. "You sure it was him?"

The man studied the picture and nodded. "Yes. That was the guy. He was a real jerk. He's not one you easily forget."

Sean thanked him and hurried to get to his plane for the next flight.

Unfortunately, David had a rock-solid alibi. Whoever attacked Emily was still unknown. Sean inwardly groaned. The longer Tom was in Alyssa's life, the bigger the danger their relationship might be rekindled. He sent up a silent prayer for God's help for all involved.

~~*~*

Tom stared at himself in the mirror. The gash across his face was healing, but the scar would remain. He was still a pretty good-looking guy.

If he was lucky, maybe people would think he'd been wounded as a war correspondent. Unfortunately, with the detective's relentless questioning and his mother's constant interference, the only battles he fought were for his own freedom.

Now that he was out of the hospital and moved to a rehab facility, maybe he'd soon be well enough to get out of this town, away from police, and away from his family. Alyssa had been the only bright spot, but even she'd kept her distance. Not that he could blame her, he'd been a jerk to leave her. But settling down had been the last thing on his mind before graduating from college.

He hobbled back to his bed and sat on the side. He had to find out what had happened to Emily. Someone had attacked her, but who and why?

His mother barged in the door. "Tom, we need to talk. That detective is still asking questions. Before your father left this morning, he told me he has hired a man to investigate what happened to Emily. I still can't believe you didn't stay as a reporter. You could be working with your father in his business instead of taking silly photos."

"Mother, I'm doing well as a photographer. I love my job."

"What kind of life is it taking pictures of *those* people? You could be writing Pulitzer-winning articles like your father. You could be living back with us in North Carolina, married to one of society's finest, and raising a little family."

"That's what you're mad about, isn't it? You

always wanted me to stay under your thumb, dating who you wanted me to date, and marrying who you wanted me to marry. It's not going to happen, Mother. You need to go home. As soon as they release me, I'm heading back to California."

She looked like he'd slapped her. "Well! If that's the thanks I get for all I've done for you, I'll just go home. You can get out of this mess yourself. Go on back to that little tramp of a girlfriend you had in college."

"*What?* What are you talking about? Alyssa was the kindest girl I've ever known. The only thing you didn't like about her is that she didn't come from the society women you hang around."

"She wasn't worthy of you." His mother dabbed at her eyes as though crying. "After all I've done for you."

"Oh, please. Save the theatrics and fake tears. Alyssa was much better than me, and she sure is better than you."

His mother's eyes narrowed. "You are so ungrateful. All I ever did was want the best for you. Alyssa wasn't who you needed. No telling *where* you would be if you had stayed with her. You needed to be with your family, with those who love you and have sacrificed so much for you."

"Just stop. Go home; I don't need you or want you here."

She opened her mouth as though to say

something, then, with a loud huff, turned on her heels and stomped away.

Exhausted, Tom leaned back on his bed. He should have done that years ago. Maybe he and Alyssa would have had a shot and made things work.

Sixteen

Disconnecting the call, Alyssa stared at the clock next to her bed. She should be getting ready to go to work for her night shift. Instead, the hospital had called to tell her to stay home. Until the investigation was over, she'd been suspended.

She wanted to scream. All her hard work in school, all the years studying to be in the medical field, and one accusation made by a vindictive woman could send it all tumbling down.

She got up and took a shower, letting the hot water wash over her. If only she could wash away the mess with Mrs. Chambers, the mess with Tom, and the mess of her past. Water turning cool, Alyssa dried off and got dressed.

Feeling like a wet rag, she made her way down the hall to get a cup of coffee.

"What are you still doing here?" Kat, now home from her day at work, hurried to her side. "Are you sick?"

"I've been suspended." The words stuck in her throat.

"Oh, no. Is that because of what Tom's mom said?"

"Yes. I am not having good thoughts about that woman."

"I'm with you. I think we should slap her. Not that it would help, but maybe it would make you feel better. It would sure make me feel better."

"Thanks, but I'll just have to wait and see what happens next."

"I'm sorry you can't work tonight." Kat paused, then grinned. "But, that means we finally have an evening together. We haven't had girl time in forever. Let's watch a movie. Grab a gallon of ice cream and drown our sorrows."

"*Our* sorrows?"

"I broke up with Stephen. He got all handsy and wanted more than I was ready to give. I'm thinking about going to a Monastery."

"You can't be a monk, and I don't see you as a nun."

"No, silly." Kat nudged her. "There's a spiritual retreat center in the mountains where people can have a quiet time to get away from everything. Want to join me?"

"That does sound nice. If I don't get my job back, I may have lots of time."

"You'll be back to work soon. They'll find out the truth."

"I hope so. I love nursing."

"How about we nurse a pizza?" Kat pointed toward the kitchen. "I have one in the freezer."

"That's my kind of nursing." She joined her

friend for a relaxing dinner followed by a bowl of ice cream.

Alyssa glanced at the time. She didn't want to get off her schedule of staying awake at night, so she knew just what she wanted to do and where she wanted to go. "I'm going to head out for a little while and take some photos."

"It's 7:00 at night. Where are you going?"

"The Bruneau Sand Dunes."

"Why? It's over an hour's drive from here, which is a little late for playing in the sand; plus, don't they close at ten during winter?"

"Yes, on all accounts, but no sandcastles on this trip. It's a great place to photograph stars since there's not much light from anything but the sky. Last year I took some great shots of the Milky Way."

"Oh, that's right. Sounds fun. Can I join you?"

"Sure. But I'm not sure how long I'll be gone."

"No worries." Kat jumped up. "If we stay late, I'll sleep in the car while you drive home. Plus, tomorrow is the weekend."

"I forgot what day it was. But, don't you usually drive to see your parents on the weekend?"

"Yep, but I'll stay in the area for you. They'll manage without me for a few days."

"Then, grab your coat and gloves while I get my tripod and camera gear. Girls' night out it is!"

"I'll make us a thermos of hot chocolate and

get a couple of blankets. This is going to be so much fun."

By the time Kat finished getting together all the things she was bringing, Alyssa's car was packed with enough jackets, food, and blankets, for a five-day excursion.

Alyssa laughed. "You crack me up. I usually don't have much with me when I go on photo shoots."

"Maybe you would enjoy your outings if you prepared as I do."

"It would be more fun, but I'd never get anything done because I'd be preparing all that needed to be prepared and then have to set it up and break it down."

"Oh well. It's a shame we work on different time shifts; I could be your roadie."

"That would be fun, but you'd starve to death since I don't make much money at this."

"Ah, well, you can pay me in the enjoyment of your company."

"Ha. Yeah, right. But, thanks for coming."

An hour and a half later, Alyssa set up her tripod and prepared her camera with her wide-angle lens and remote shutter release. She then turned and watched in amazement as Kat laid out blankets, a picnic basket, mugs for their hot drinks, and two chairs for relaxing.

Kat waved her hand as though displaying a work of art. "This is the way you should be taking photos."

"It sure beats my normal setup."

"Is there anything else I can do to help as you take your prize-winning photographs?"

"Grab some hot chocolate and sit back and enjoy the view of God's starry sky."

Kat sat, sipped her hot cocoa, and gazed at the stars. "It's beautiful." Her voice quiet, reverent.

After setting everything up on her camera and starting the autotimer, Alyssa sat next to her friend. The stars seemed to burst from the sky on the moonless night. "Can you imagine how many millions and billions of stars, galaxies, and incredible things are out there?."

"It really is awesome. It's hard to imagine we're spinning through space. I'm grateful gravity holds us on earth."

"Me too. But, I feel like my life is spinning out of control with the mess with Tom, his mom, and now the possibility of losing my job."

"I'm sorry. I know it's hard." Kat pointed at the sky. "Just remember that God, who made all these stars, can keep you together, and he'll take care of you."

"I know that in my heart, but my head hasn't been very restful. I just wish I could go back in time and change everything. I'd never have dated Tom, and I'd restart my life from day one."

"Really? Do you think you would want to do that?"

"Wouldn't you?" Alyssa asked.

"Maybe? No." Kat shook her head. "I don't

think so. I think I would just have made other mistakes. If things changed, I would never have learned the lessons I learned."

"I guess that's true. But I would love to erase several things in my past."

"Me too, friend. Me too."

They sat in silence. Alyssa stared into the night, wishing she could see into heaven and find the answers to all her questions. If she could turn back time, what would that have meant? What would she have changed?

She would have been better at trusting God, enjoying life more, and worrying so much about the future. She would have stuck up for herself as a kid and been braver and stronger. In college, she'd never have dated Tom.

Then again, would she have been the same person? What if she wouldn't have met Sean?

"I take what I said earlier back," Kat said. "If given the opportunity, I would change one main thing. I would have fallen in love with God earlier, early enough to keep me from being swayed by the love of people." Kat hesitated for a moment. "Alyssa, you know some things about me, but lots happened when I was growing up, things I don't talk about."

Even in the darkness, Alyssa could see tears rimmed in Kat's eyes. "I'm so sorry. I'm here for you anytime you want to share."

"Not tonight. Maybe someday. Let's just say without God; I wouldn't have made it."

Alyssa leaned close to Kat. "I'm sorry I

haven't been a better friend. I've been pretty self-absorbed, especially lately."

"Don't worry. You're a great friend. Right now, I'm here for you. Now, get up and take some great pictures of this amazing sky."

Alyssa inwardly kicked herself as she stood and took more photos. She'd known Kat for over a year, and when she thought about it, she still knew very little about her. Kat was always upbeat, seemed to have the world at her feet, and Alyssa had never stopped to consider Kat's life hadn't always been easy.

"We can't change the past, but we can change today." Kat's quiet voice hung in the night air. "We can change how we view things."

Alyssa turned to her friend. "But changing how we view things in light of the past is hard."

"Sure, it is, yet the things we go through are only part of our story. Some people stay locked in their past, replaying their tragedies, their heartache and pain, and never move forward. They miss what is happening in the present and what will happen in the future. God offers freedom, forgiveness, and new beginnings. What we give to God frees us, makes us stronger, becomes part of our epic adventure." Kat stood next to her. "Hey, you know you are going to get a happy ending with God, so be brave in your story."

"You sure are getting deep tonight. Maybe you should write a book."

Kat just smiled.

At 9:30, they packed up and headed back to the townhouse. Nothing might have changed in her situation, but Alyssa did feel better. The conversations they had made her think and try to reprocess her life.

Once they returned home, Kat went to bed, and Alyssa went to her room. What if she saw things in her past as only stepping stones to who she was and who she was becoming? Thinking of her life as an epic adventure did make her smile.

She couldn't change her past, the things others said and did, and the things she did or didn't do, but she did have today. She needed to remember those truths, live in the moment, trust God, and step out with bravery.

Her positive thoughts came to an abrupt halt when Mrs. Chambers came to mind. The accusation made by that woman was all so unfair. *Ugh.* How could she go from feeling on top of the world to being slammed dunk in anger?

The Bible verse came to mind, *Pray for those who persecute you.* Why in the world would she think of that verse? Then again, that's probably where that came from - way beyond the world.

Maybe there was more to that verse, something that would give her an out when it came to Mrs. Chambers. She grabbed her phone and opened the Bible software to search. Matthew 5:44 jumped out at her. Jesus said, *But*

I say to you, love your enemies and pray for those who persecute you,

That was worse than just praying. Why, and *how* was she supposed to love and pray for the woman who was trying to ruin her life?

Seventeen

Sun barely peeking over the horizon, Alyssa kept thinking about the Bible verse she read earlier. She still couldn't pray for Mrs. Chambers, and she sure didn't feel like loving her.

Alyssa did pray for God to help her with all of that, but she felt like a pouting toddler not ready to give in to what God would want her to do. Praying for someone that willingly did something to hurt someone didn't make sense. Couldn't she just be mad?

Then she remembered a woman who had lived down the street from her family's house. Mrs. Freedman was gorgeous and looked like a fashion model in her younger days. Even though the woman's name was Freedman, she didn't live free. She stayed mad at her ex-husband, angry at her neighbors, furious at her family, blamed everyone for her problems, and refused to forgive anyone. Over the years, Mrs. Freedman's looks dissolved into a hardened, angry shell of her former beauty.

Alyssa shuddered. Staying mad at Mrs. Chambers didn't help anything or anyone.

Tiptoeing down the hall, Alyssa left a note

for whenever Kat woke up, then grabbed her coat and camera gear and headed to her car.

Her conversation with the couple she'd met the other day came to mind. Their invitation for her to drop by anytime seemed genuine. Perhaps they'd allow her to take photos of the river on their property. And maybe, just maybe, they would have some words of advice that would help.

Even though her thoughts were racing, the quiet morning and light traffic made her trip easy. Before she knew it, she drove down the driveway to the Wright's house.

Alyssa stepped out of her car and hesitated. Maybe she shouldn't have come. What would they think about her just showing up? Good grief, why didn't she call or at least text?

Mrs. Wright walked out on her porch and waved. "I had a feeling you would be coming over. I made cinnamon biscuits and have a pot of coffee ready. Robert's working in his workshop out back. Come on in."

"You thought I would be coming? I don't know whether to be a little worried or grateful." Alyssa followed her to the dining table and took off her jacket.

Mrs. Wright chuckled. "Don't worry. It's just that your face kept coming to mind when I was praying. I was worried about you." She took the goodies out of the oven and served two on a plate for each of them. "Help yourself to some coffee."

Thanking her, Alyssa fixed her a mug of java and sat across from her kind, new friend. "I just stopped by to see if you'd let me take a few photos by the river."

"You are always welcome to do that. After we eat, I'll show you some perfect spots. Since you're here, and if you feel comfortable, please tell me what's going on and how can I help?"

Alyssa took a sip of coffee. How could Mrs. Wright even think she might be coming to visit? Was that weird or a God-thing? "Um, you kind of caught me off guard. I just had a rough couple of days." She paused. Maybe coming here wasn't just a spur-of-the-moment idea or an accident. She needed Godly advice. "Do you know the verse about loving and praying for your enemies?"

"Yes, that can be a tough one. However, there is a way to do that regardless of how we feel."

"This I want to hear."

Mrs. Wright sat straight, her eyes sparkling. "Okay, Jesus said to love our enemies, pray for those who persecute us, even to bless them. Jesus also said if we do not forgive others, then we won't be forgiven."

"Ouch, that's hard," Alyssa said. "I want to be forgiven, but I'll be honest, it's hard when it comes to one lady who made my life miserable in the past and is trying to get me in trouble now."

"May I share some advice?" At Alyssa's nod,

Mrs. Wright continued. "Turn the prayers around. We pray for others because Jesus prays and intercedes for us. And the nice thing is that means He will help us as we pray. We also can bless others because we are so blessed to know God's grace and be God's children. We forgive others because God forgave us. So, you can pray for that woman that God blesses her to know God's love, that God will bless her to see God's truth and turn from her wicked ways, and that God blesses her hard heart with a heart sensitive and open to His love."

"That's good. All that makes sense, but loving our enemies doesn't make sense and is so hard. I can say something about loving someone, but God knows I do *not* love that woman."

"I understand. However, when God's love is in us, we can freely love others. Even when someone is unlovely, we can love them with God's love. It's *his* love, so it's a supernatural thing. It's another beautiful way that the world living in darkness can see the light of Christ." Mrs. Wright stopped talking for a moment. "Oh, dear. I'm sorry I get so excited when I talk about God. Please forgive me if I'm rambling."

The back door opened and slammed. Mr. Wright, holding his hand, said a quick hello, ran past them and disappeared down the hallway.

"Robert?" Mrs. Wright rose to her feet and followed her husband.

A few minutes later, Mrs. Wright hurried to Alyssa. "Could I borrow you for a moment?

Robert cut his hand, and I'm not sure if he needs stitches."

Hurrying down the hall, Alyssa stepped inside the bathroom where Mr. Wright, holding his bloody hand, gave her a sheepish grin. "I'm usually not this accident-prone."

"We washed it off, but it keeps bleeding." Mrs. Wright added.

Alyssa examined the wound. Fortunately, the cut wasn't too deep. However, it did run from the palm of his hand to the edge of his fingers. "How did you do this?"

"Well, I was holding a piece of wood for the project I'm working on and needed to shave off a little on the side. The knife kinda slipped."

"I think you'll be okay. Let's get it cleaned off and keep applying pressure. Do you have any bandages?"

Mrs. Wright handed her a box full of medical supplies. "We keep well-stocked since we live outside of town."

Alyssa found everything needed to clean and properly bandage his wound. "You should be fine. Just take good care of yourself until this heals."

"Thank you, Nurse Alyssa." Mr. Wright cradled his hand. "We owe you."

"Of course. I'm glad I could help." Alyssa turned to Mrs. Wright. "You were going to tell me something that happened?"

"Oh, yes. That's right. Robert, would you like to join us?"

"Sure. A cinnamon biscuit will help in my healing." He grinned as he walked to the kitchen.

After getting another cup of coffee, Alyssa sat across from the couple.

Mrs. Wright turned to her husband. "Robert, I hope you don't mind me sharing what happened a few years ago."

"Nope, not at all." He paused. "Then again, what were you sharing?"

"About your job."

"Oh, that one. Go ahead. We know what happened on the other side."

"A few years ago, Robert lost his job because of a co-worker lying about him. It was a horrible time. All the accusations were untrue, and eventually the truth came to light, and Robert was vindicated, but the year-long battle was awful, terrible, and heart-wrenching."

"I'm so sorry," Alyssa said.

"It was pretty rough." Mr. Wright added. "But God did amazing things. Romans 8:28 is true; all things work together for good to those who love God, to those who are the called according to his purpose. I wouldn't want to go through something like that again, but God did not waste a moment of our time or pain."

"Alyssa." Mrs. Wright waited until she looked her way. "God has you in His loving hands. Whatever is going on, God has a plan and purpose. Stay close to him, keep praying, and trust him. Something good will come."

Alyssa sat back in her chair, let their words sink deep and attach to her soul like stepping stones leading her forward. She knew God is good, and she believed in the promises in the Bible. What she didn't know was what would happen next and how long the battle with Mrs. Chambers would continue. Yet, inside her, a feeling rose up that something bigger was going on than she could see, that the struggle she was in wasn't just about her. The hair on the back of her neck prickled as an energy rose in her spirit, preparing her to be ready.

Mrs. Wright smiled. "I don't know what God has planned for you, but the thought comes for you to remember to be ready because the battle belongs to the Lord."

Alyssa rubbed the goosebumps from her arms. "You must have been reading my mind. I feel like something is coming. But, I'm not afraid, and I almost feel like I've been given a covering of some sort."

"Oh my, I read something just this morning I have got to share with you." Mrs. Wright hurried to get her Bible where it lay open on the couch. Returning, she sat next to Alyssa. "This is from Isaiah 61:10; I will greatly rejoice in the Lord, my soul shall be joyful in my God; for He has clothed me with the garments of salvation, He has covered me with the robe of righteousness." Mrs. Wright gazed at Alyssa. "Whatever God is doing in your life; he wants you to know he's got you covered."

Alyssa rubbed the moisture from her eyes. "I can't believe we are having a conversation like this. I barely know you."

"We may just have met the other day, but the Holy Spirit knows who belongs to the Lord, and he quickly connects hearts through his love."

"Thank you." She sat, thinking, pondering, wondering about the conversation, all that was said. "I guess I better let you have your morning. I need to get back home and catch some sleep. I hope the hospital will let me come back to work soon."

"They will. Have faith." Mr. Wright grinned and nodded.

Mrs. Wright pointed toward the back door. "Did you want to take photos by the river?"

Alyssa checked the time. "Maybe I will come back another day. I have lots to think about."

"You are welcome anytime." Mrs. Wright led her to the door and hugged her. "It's going to be okay. We will be praying for you."

On the way home, Alyssa contemplated the conversation and the amazing feeling she had of almost being a warrior prepared for battle. Fighting didn't sound like a good thing, but being prepared was an incredible feeling.

While thanking God, she noticed her car gas level was low. Once she arrived in the Boise area, she stopped at the first gas station and hopped out to fill her tank.

A black car with heavily tinted windows pulled in at the pump next to hers. The driver's side door opened, and a dark-haired guy with mirrored sunglasses stepped out. He leaned down to talk to whoever was still inside the vehicle. "Make it quick and get back here." His deep voice seethed anger.

The passenger door opened, and a blonde-haired woman wrapped a coat around her as she ran to the building.

Trying to act like she didn't notice, Alyssa finished gassing her car and then pulled her vehicle to a parking space in front of the convenience store area. Something wasn't right. She felt repelled by the guy and compelled to see if the woman needed help.

Alyssa made her way to the restroom. The door opened, and she stood face-to-face with a woman who was the spitting image of Emily Kingston.

Eighteen

"Emily?" Alyssa blocked her path. "Is it you?"

The woman's mouth fell open, and she stepped back. "No, it's not." She raised the hood of her jacket, covering part of her face. "I.... I just look like her."

Alyssa moved closer, keeping her voice low. "Oh, well, if you *were* Emily. I'd want you to know that Tom Chambers was hurt when his car crashed as he was trying to rescue you. And, he is being questioned by the police about your disappearance."

The color drained from the woman's face, and for a moment, she stood quiet. "I'm not her, okay." She pushed Alyssa aside and ran out the door.

It had to be Emily. Alyssa hurried to follow to see if she could get the car's license plate.

Alyssa stepped outside. The black SUV barely stopped to let the woman inside; the vehicle's tires squealed as the car disappeared into city traffic.

Taking a deep breath to steady herself, Alyssa tried to remember the few numbers and letters she had seen on the license plate. Taking her phone out of her pocket, she ran to her car to find the detective's phone number that had questioned Tom.

Hands shaking, she dialed the number. The call went to his voice mail. She left a message quickly explaining what she'd seen and left her phone number.

Alyssa then dialed Tom's number. As soon as he answered, she told him what happened and to send the investigator his father had hired. Tom gasped, thanked her, and hung up.

She took a deep breath. What if she was wrong? What if that wasn't Emily? Maybe it was someone who just looked like her? Alyssa replayed the scene in her mind. No, it had to be Emily, and her reaction to hearing about Tom seemed to be a genuine surprise.

Alyssa answered her ringing phone. The detective's voice asked her again what she had seen. He explained a police unit was in the area, and an officer was on the way to question her.

Alyssa prayed like crazy, asking for God's help.

Pulse racing, she leaned her head against her steering wheel to try and calm down. Why didn't she try to follow the car? *Argh!*

A rap on her car window made her jump.

An officer stood outside. "Alyssa Nelson?" At her nod, he continued. "Could you step outside your car for a moment?"

She complied and stood next to the man's towering frame.

He leveled his gaze on her. "Tell me everything you saw and heard."

Before she could reply, the detective she'd met at the hospital walked toward them and addressed the other officer. "I'll take it from here. Would you go in and question the station attendants and anyone else who may have been inside?"

The officer nodded and left.

"Since it's cold, let's step inside the building." The detective motioned for her to follow him. "Tell me everything you saw and heard."

They moved to a quiet spot in the back, and Alyssa relayed everything she could remember.

His gaze surveyed her face. "When the woman put up her hood, did you see her right hand?"

"I wasn't paying attention to her hands."

"This is important. When she raised her hood, did you see anything on her fingers?"

Alyssa closed her eyes, prayed God would help her remember, and replayed the scene in her mind. Her eyes flew open. "I did see something. On her pinky finger, there was a big, tear-dropped shape ruby ring."

The detective nodded. "Good work. It sounds like Emily Kingston is on the run."

The police officer hurried toward them. "We have video, sir. It does look like it was David and Emily."

The detective thanked Alyssa and told her

he would be in touch.

Dismissed, but wishing she could stay and hear what would happen next, she went to her car and buckled in to return home.

Another rap on her window made her jump. Good grief, she was jumpy.

When she rolled down her window, a man held up a business card. "Are you Alyssa Nelson?" At her tentative nod, he continued. "I'm the investigator for Tom Chambers. He called to let me know what was going on. Can you fill me in on what you saw?"

Alyssa explained again what she had seen. He took notes, thanked her, and went inside the station.

Her adrenaline still pumping, she placed a call to Sean and left him a message. How she wished he was here with her. And one more person needed to know what else she'd found out; she placed her next call to Tom.

~~*~*

Hitting the wall with his fist, Tom disconnected the call from Alyssa. Had Emily framed him? Was it all for a stupid publicity stunt? Why would she do that to him?

He rubbed his aching hand as all the frustration, pain, and anger came out. Hobbling over to his rehab hospital room window, he looked out at the distant hills. Maybe now the police would believe him, and he could get his life back. Now perhaps this nightmare would be over.

Still, no matter what happened, he had to do one more thing. Before he left, he needed to see Alyssa again. He should never have let her go.

Nineteen

He'd always dreamed of living in a cabin by the river. The house closing finalized, Sean walked the small plot of land he had just purchased overlooking the Big Wood River near Hailey, Idaho. He stopped and paused next to the river.

He still couldn't believe the incredibly generous offer the grandparents of one of the children he had flown had made. In gratitude for Sean's flying the family back and forth as their granddaughter received medical treatment, they'd given him the option to buy a little fishing cabin they no longer used.

The family wanted to make sure whoever had the property would be someone they would want as neighbors and who would take care of that portion of the land they'd held for generations.

He never thought he could buy something in the area since most of the property in the vicinity went for millions. Although the amount they offered wasn't cheap, he'd always been careful with his money, and with the help of an inheritance from his grandparents and a modest loan, he would make it work.

Unlocking the door to the cabin, he stepped inside. The 1400 square-foot, three-bedroom, two-bath log home had been built in 1945 and renovated in the early 1990s. Sun streamed from the large windows highlighting the well-worn wood floors. The main living area contained a vaulted beamed ceiling, and a wood-burning stove stood in one corner. The house also had a decent-sized kitchen with enough room for a small table. Outside, the back deck overlooked the river.

He planned to refinish the hardwood floors, paint the bedrooms, and buy new appliances and countertops. For the rest of the work, he could hire someone to help him get the cabin finished.

In gratitude to God, Sean fell to his knees for answering his prayers. Yet one prayer remained unanswered. He hoped and prayed to have Alyssa as his wife.

The time went swiftly as he prayed and thanked God. When his knees began aching, he stood and glanced at his watch. He had one more stop he wanted to make before he needed to get to the airport. He'd be busy the next couple of weeks, but when he returned, he would move and start the renovations and then make time to visit Alyssa.

~~*~*

Alyssa rode the elevator to Tom's third-floor room at the rehab hospital. The message he'd left on her phone said he had urgent news.

Opening the door, she peeked in. Thankfully, Tom was the only one in the room. The gash on his face now fainter, his arm in a sling, and his leg still in a brace, he hobbled toward her.

"Thanks for coming." He motioned with his good arm to the chair in the corner. "Please, sit. I need to talk to you." He waited until she sat, then stabilized himself against his bed. "I'm sorry about what happened with my mother. And, I'm not just talking about the incident at the hospital. I'm sorry about the way she interfered in our relationship. And, I'm sorry for the way I treated you."

"Thank you. But I think we just weren't meant to be."

"What if we were?" Moisture rimmed his eyes, and his gaze surveyed her. "I was an idiot to let you go. Look, I know I messed up. I'm sorry. Maybe we could give things another chance?

Alyssa's heart whimpered and folded in on itself. She had to stay strong, not let him get to her. She wasn't the same insecure girl she'd been in college. The past couldn't be changed, and she had been given a new opportunity. She shook her head. "Tom, I'm seeing someone."

He nodded and blew out a breath. "Story of my life. Always too late to get the lady."

Before she could say anything, a muscular,

dark-haired man with military-cut hair stepped inside the room.

He pushed a wheelchair forward. "Tom Chambers, time for rehab."

"Really? I just finished an hour ago."

The man stepped toward him. "We've got to work on a few more things."

"That's weird. They said I was done for the day."

"Things change." He grabbed Tom and shoved him into the chair. "Come on."

Alyssa bristled at the brusqueness of the nurse. "You sure are pushy."

The man's dark eyes surveyed her. "What's it to you?"

"I'm a nurse. We do not handle patients like this."

The man shrugged. "Whatever."

Tom reached out to Alyssa. "Will I see you again?"

"I don't know. Probably not."

"Keep my number, okay? If things change with whoever you are seeing, give me a call."

She nodded. Emotions collided as memories bounced through her mind; Alyssa waited until they left. She had stood up for herself. She could almost see her heart standing tall, brave, and beating stronger.

Then a thought hit her. The nurse that took Tom wore military-looking boots. Why would a guy dressed in scrubs be wearing something like that? Plus, he didn't wear a name tag or hospital identification. Maybe something else was going on.

She raced down the hall just as the elevator doors closed. Turning around, she noticed another nurse coming out of a patient's room. "Excuse me. Do you know who is doing rehab on Tom Chambers?"

"I just finished an hour ago. He should be back in his room."

"No, some guy just came to get him. He didn't have an ID, and he was wearing military boots. Would you please call security? I'm going to take the stairs."

The nurse gave her a quizzical expression. "I'm not sure that's necessary."

"Please, something's going on that's not good. Tom witnessed a crime and may be in danger."

The nurse quickly grabbed her cell phone and placed a call.

Alyssa ran down the stairwell to the first floor. The elevator was already open when she arrived, and people were boarding. She twirled around, looking for Tom and the man. They were nowhere to be seen.

She ran to the front door, then down a hall to the back door. A white paneled van pulled out, but no one was in the area. *Where did they go?*

Desperate, she dialed Tom's number. A ringtone sounded down the hall. Running as fast as she could, she followed the sound and stopped at a trash can.

Peering inside the container, she found Tom's phone sitting on the top of the garbage.

Twenty

Hours later, hungry, and exhausted, Alyssa arrived at her townhouse. She'd talked to the security people at the rehab hospital, the detective, the police, and Tom's private investigator. The video at the hospital had confirmed the man with Tom was not a hospital employee, and the white van had been the one that took Tom. An APB had been issued to find Tom, the suspect, and the van.

Why hadn't she asked more questions of the man? Why didn't she follow him, write down the van's license plate, or do something more than just letting Tom be taken?

Alyssa kicked off her shoes and collapsed on her couch. She'd never felt more alone; Kat was at work, and Sean was away flying in various cities. Even though he had called and texted, it wasn't the same. She wanted Sean here with her.

Her conversation with Mrs. Wright about everything working out for good seemed to be a lifetime ago. Nothing good seemed to be happening; she was still suspended, and Tom had been kidnapped and was out there somewhere. At least she hoped he was still out there. *Oh, God.* What if something happened to him? What if she should have done more?

Alyssa fell to her knees and prayed for Tom's protection, for wisdom for the police, and wisdom for her. She prayed for Tom's parents and then even zeroed down her prayers for comfort and peace for Tom's mom.

Alyssa groaned, moaned, and tears fell while she prayed. Then her heart cracked open to forgive Tom for what he had done in their relationship, forgive herself for doing things she knew were wrong, and even forgive Mrs. Chambers.

An invisible weight filled with bitterness, anger, and shame, dropped from Alyssa's shoulders, and disappeared in the light of God's grace and mercy. Her tears now held relief and cleansing as she thanked God and continued to pray.

~~*~*

An excruciating, burning pain shot through Tom's arm. Groaning, he opened his eyes. Head groggy, focus wavy, he tried to clear his head. The last thing he remembered was being taken to physical therapy by some big, military-looking guy. The man had wheeled him on the elevator and then given him a shot. Tom remembered asking why, and the guy had just smiled. No other memories came.

Where was he? Tom tried to still himself,

concentrate, focus on his environment. His hands were agonizingly zip-tied behind his back, legs zip-tied at his ankles, and he laid on his side on an old bare mattress. The musty-smelling room was empty except for the bed. Wide-planked wooden floorboards, the walls clapboard, made him wonder if he was in an old cabin. Faint sounds of birds calling to one another came from outside a boarded window.

A dim light came from under the door. Wherever he had been taken was silent. Trying to regulate his breathing, he tried to calm down. How long had he been here? Had the guy kidnapped him and just left him somewhere to die? Or would he be back to kill him off or torture him?

Desperate for help, Tom prayed God would help him to escape or that someone would come to his rescue. He hadn't been on speaking terms with God for years, not because of anything bad that happened in his life, but basically because he knew he hadn't lived right. Was he being paid back for the times he had been a jerk to other people? The times he had lied to women?

When he had worked as a journalist, he'd done some rotten things to Bethany Davis to get a story. When he dated Alyssa, he hadn't treated her right. A painful list of his many other indiscretions flashed in his mind.

People said their life stories played out before they died. *Was he going to die?* Wait a minute, if people had actually died, how would anyone know their life flashed before their eyes?

Hot tears rolled down his cheek. Guys weren't supposed to cry, but who made that stupid rule anyway. He had tons of regrets, things he wished he would have done differently. If only he could go back and change his past.

If he was going to meet his maker, he better be prepared. What was he thinking? He couldn't die, *wouldn't* die. He had to think, plan, do something. He needed to live. He begged God to give him another chance.

The sound of a vehicle's tires crunched on gravel outside the window. His heart lodged in his throat. Someone was coming.

Twenty-one

The front door opened. "Hello!" Kat's voice came down the hall, followed by the click-clack of her high heels. She stopped beside Alyssa. "You still off work?"

"Yeah, I'm still waiting to hear back."

"Any word on Tom?" Her friend kicked off her heels and sat next to her.

Alyssa spent the next thirty minutes filling in her roommate on all that had happened.

"Wow, that's a lot. We still have a few hours of daylight left. Want to go on a Tom hunt?"

"I wish, but we wouldn't have a clue where to look."

"Good point." Kat tapped her manicured finger on her chin. "The police probably have a much better idea what to do. I bet they checked those traffic camera thingies to see if the van went somewhere. Maybe they even have drones flying looking for him. If an evil fan, or Emily and her boyfriend are behind this, why would they want to kidnap Tom? Maybe it's something else. Maybe his evil mom did something to someone, and that someone is trying to get back at her family."

"I already have enough rattling around in my

brain without worrying about all those additional things."

"Sorry, I guess I watch too many cop shows. Speaking of cops, I have a good buddy on the police force; want me to call him?"

Alyssa hesitated for only a moment. "Yes. Find out anything you can."

Kat placed the call and stepped down the hall. From the tone of the first part of the conversation, the guy was very happy to hear from her. Twenty-two long minutes later, her roommate hurried back to her side. "Okay, here's the latest. The hospital video camera showed Tom taken into the elevator, given a shot, then driven away in a white van. Plus, they do have traffic cams and know which way the van was heading. They recognized the guy who took Tom. He's a two-bit criminal who does all sorts of odd jobs, none of which are above the law. Anywho, they narrowed the search to near Idaho City. The bad guy has a family cabin up that way. The police are already on their way."

"I thought the police were supposed to be quiet about things like that."

Kat smiled and blushed. "I guess I just have that gift."

"Either way, I hope your friend is right, and they find Tom soon. If anything happened to him..." Alyssa's breath caught. "I'd feel like it was my fault."

"Why would you think that?"

"I was in his room when that man took Tom.

I should have noticed more, followed, made sure he was okay."

"You couldn't have known. Plus, if you had followed them, the guy might have taken you, and then no one would have a clue what happened. The only reason the police know Tom has been kidnapped is because you were there to report it."

"I guess so."

"I know so. Don't carry guilt you don't have to carry. Most people haul enough guilt baggage without taking on additional. So, instead of sitting here beating yourself up, pray. God knows where Tom is. God knows where that guy is. God knows what's going on with Emily, David, and the whole mess." Kat surveyed her for a moment. "Hey, are you having renewed feelings for heartbreak, Tommy boy?"

"No, definitely not. It's over, done, finished; I am moving on. I just want him safe."

Kat's gaze surveyed her for a moment. "Okay, good. Just checking."

"Plus, there's someone else."

"Really? Do tell."

"Sean."

"Sean?" Kat's smile was wide. "The buddy you've known forever, Sean?"

"One and the same." Alyssa smiled at the thought. "He's turned into a mighty fine man."

"Well, look at you. You've been busy behind my back. I'm proud of you for taking a step into the dating pool again."

"I just hope my heart doesn't drown."

"Nope. Not going to happen. I have good feelings about Sean. Always have. I haven't seen him in a few months, but I always liked him. Plus, he's cute."

"He is, isn't he?" Alyssa paused, shook her head, trying to clear her thoughts. "I probably shouldn't be talking about happy things when Tom is still missing and in danger."

"It's okay to talk about good things even when bad things are happening. Bad things are always going to be happening until we get to heaven."

"Just feels wrong or something."

"It's not wrong to notice good things. The devil wants us all to be depressed, worried, and only focusing on bad things instead of being thankful to God for everything good."

"I can be thankful and grateful for Sean, but it still doesn't make things right for Tom."

Kat hugged her. "I'm sorry. I do hope he'll be okay."

"Me too." All those years she'd spent with Tom, then spent worrying about the time spent with Tom, and the difficulties she had with his mom welled up and spilled out. Alyssa let the tears flow as her friend held her. Oh, how she hoped and prayed Tom would be okay.

An hour later, back in her room, Alyssa lay on her bed praying, thinking, worrying about what had happened, what might happen, and what would happen if her worst fears did happen. *Ack!* She was going to go crazy, absolutely bonkers if she didn't stop her brain from whirling out of control.

She checked the time. Maybe she should call the Wrights and ask them to pray. Tom needed prayers, and she needed help calming down.

Alyssa placed the call, and the words flowed as she told Mrs. Wright everything about what was happening and had happened. Alyssa even mentioned Sean and how she hoped everything would work out with him.

Mrs. Wright listened, prayed with her, prayed for her, and gently reminded Alyssa about the verse in Philippians four.

Feeling better, Alyssa thanked her and picked up her Bible. Finding the verse, she read, *Be anxious for nothing, but in everything by prayer and supplication, with thanksgiving, let your requests be made known to God; and the peace of God, which surpasses all understanding, will guard your hearts and minds through Christ Jesus.*

It sounded easy, but it wasn't. Anxiousness was a part of life, and being anxious about this situation seemed to be the only thing she knew how to do. Good grief, even her prayers had been anxious.

The verse said prayer, supplication, and thanksgiving. Prayer made sense. She could do that, but being thankful was difficult during tough times. Yet thanksgiving also made sense since God had all the answers because he was the answer to everything and knew everything.

But what was supplication? She searched through online Bible applications and dictionaries to help her understand. Best she could tell, supplication meant asking, seeking, and making a definite request.

Alyssa got down on her knees by her bed. "God, thank you that I can come to you. Thank you that you know all things, you know where Tom is, and you know how he can be found. God, thank you that you care for me and you care for Tom. Heavenly Father, please send someone to rescue Tom. Please help him feel you are near and fill him with your peace. I ask for your hedge of protection around him and that he will be returned safe and sound. Thank you, God. And, I ask these things in the name of Jesus Christ, your Son, who has all authority in heaven and earth. Amen."

Taking a deep breath, she blew out all the anxiety and worry and left everything in God's hands.

Her cellphone rang. Without checking the caller-id, Alyssa grabbed her phone. She relaxed at the familiar voice. Carla relayed to Alyssa her suspension was over. The hospital had talked to Mr. Jensen and finished their investigation; Alyssa was cleared to return to work tomorrow night. Breathing a sigh of relief, she thanked her supervisor, then filled her in on the latest and asked her to pray for Tom.

Alyssa ended the call and thanked God. One prayer answered, and hopefully soon, she'd hear something positive about Tom.

~~*~*

Tom held his breath, fought to silence his drumming heartbeat as the sound of heavy footsteps drew closer.

The door opened, a light flicked on, and his kidnapper, with gun in hand, stood in front of him. "About time you woke up. We're going to take a little walk. Sit up." The man took a knife from his pocket and sliced off the zip-tie from Tom's legs, then jerked him to his feet.

Tom yelped in pain. His legs felt like thousands of needles running up and down as nerve endings awakened. He stumbled and tried to stay upright. Wishing he had good legs so he could run, Tom hobbled forward.

"Move it." Grabbing Tom's arm, military man shoved him out the door, down the hall, and out a door leading outside, then jammed the gun in Tom's ribs. "Now, just a little walk through the woods, and it will all be over."

Tom swallowed the boulder-sized lump in his throat. "Over?"

"You're in the way." As he leaned close to Tom's face, the man's breath reeked of alcohol. "It's time you got out of the way. Permanently out of the way."

Vision tunneling, Tom wavered and tried to

stay on his feet.

"No, you don't. No fainting." The man grabbed Tom by his good arm and drug him through the woods.

The scream came from some desperate, primordial location as pain ripped through Tom's shoulders, his fractured arm, the zip-tie digging into his wrists, and his messed-up leg.

"Shut up! Shut up! *Shut up!*" The man dropped Tom in the dirt, kicked him in the ribs, and then got in his face. "Not one more word, not one more whimper, or I'm going to shoot you right here and right now. Get up!"

Trying to catch his breath, trying not to throw up, Tom struggled to use his good leg to help his bad leg get to his feet. He couldn't do it. He was going to die. "God forgive me."

"Man up, you sniveling sissy." Raising his gun, he moved behind Tom.

Heart pounding in his ears, Tom closed his eyes.

Stars exploded. Agonizing, excruciating pain, his breath gurgled in his throat.

Tom felt his body being dragged across the ground as blackness engulfed.

Twenty-two

Choking back tears, Alyssa stared at Tom's lifeless body. Machines silently monitored his progress. He was going to make it. His progress would be slow, but he was going to make it.

Tom's arm and leg had both been reinjured, and he had a concussion from evidently being pistol-whipped in the back of the head. The poor guy couldn't seem to get a break.

She laid her hand on his good arm and prayed for his recovery. Part of her still cared for Tom, but she knew without a doubt she loved Sean.

Tom's eyes fluttered open, and he turned toward her. "I'm alive?"

"Yes." She patted his arm. "You made it."

"I thought I was a goner." Tears ran down his face. "Did I get shot in the head?"

"No, you have a concussion from being hit in the head."

"Oh man, I thought I was dead for sure. Did they get him?"

"The police got the kidnapper. The man was killed when he shot at the police."

Tom's chest heaved as he moaned. "That was awful. I prayed, Alyssa. I really prayed."

"I was praying for you too." She reached up and moved a stray hair from his forehead. All those years, they had been together, and now only healthy non-romantic feelings remained. "I'm glad you're okay."

"I'm so sorry for how I treated you. So sorry." His voice broke in a sob.

The door to the room slammed open, and his parents rushed to his side.

Alyssa rose to her feet and stepped back.

"How is he?" Tom's father looked at his son and then addressed her.

"He's going to be okay."

Mrs. Chambers shoved Alyssa aside and sat in the chair next to Tom. "I can't believe all these bad things keep happening to you. You need to come home." She pointed at her husband. "You need to make him come home with us."

Mr. Chambers shook his head. "He's an adult; he can make his own decisions."

"Obviously, his decisions have been terrible. Just look at him!"

Tom's face flamed red. The monitor showed Tom's heart rate increasing.

Alyssa stepped forward. "Mrs. Chambers, perhaps you could discuss this outside the room."

"Why are you here?" The disdain in her voice was unmistakable. "I thought I took care of you."

"I work here."

Mr. Chambers stepped closer to his wife. "What do you mean you took care of her?"

The woman turned away from her husband. "Nothing."

His gaze rested on Alyssa. "Could you step outside for a moment? Tom, I'll be right back." He then turned to his wife. "Stay here." His command firm.

Alyssa followed him into the hallway. "Mr. Chambers, it's okay. I know you're both upset with everything that's happened."

The big man towered over her. "I don't know what she did, but I apologize." He reached in his billfold and took out his business card. "If you ever have any trouble or need help with anything, you call me." He placed his hand on her shoulder. "I always hoped you and Tom would be together."

Alyssa gulped, nodded, excused herself, and hurried back to the nurse's station. Why did she keep getting dragged into Tom's life? Was she missing something? Maybe God kept Tom around because he *had* changed, and she needed to be open to something new. Yes, she loved Sean but did she love him because he had been such a big part of her life?

"Alyssa?" Tania stood next to her. "Are you okay?"

"It's Tom again. It's all so confusing."

"May I make a suggestion?" Tania paused and waited until she had her attention. "Right now, you have been given the opportunity to come back to work. So, continue being a nurse. And remember, when in an emotional situation, don't let feelings get away from you. Tom was an old flame, so make sure if a flame sparks again, it's not fueled only by emotions or because he's injured. You know the truth of what went on with him and his family. Step back, take a breath, and remember what you already know, what you've seen with your own eyes, and what you have already experienced. And Alyssa, please don't pursue a relationship that doesn't bring life, Godly life. Talk to God and let Him guide you." Tania hugged her. "I'm here if you need me. And I'll make sure to take over Tom's care while he's with us."

Alyssa thanked her friend. She needed not to let her emotions run away with her. She knew the truth, Tom had not been good for her in college, and even if he had changed, he wasn't the one she needed to be with now.

Twenty-three

Back home, half-asleep, Alyssa fumbled to find her phone and brought it to her ear.

"It's me. I need your help." Tom's voice sounded desperate. "Please come back to the hospital."

She sat up in bed and checked the time. What was happening now? "I'll be right there."

She took a quick shower, got ready for work, and ran to the kitchen to grab a protein bar or something quick to eat.

Kat, in her pajamas, came around the corner. "Hey, are you going to work early?"

"No, yes. Tom called, and he said he needed my help."

"Seriously? Again? What's going on this time?"

"I'm not sure, but I've never heard his voice like that."

"I don't like it. I think you need to put more distance between him."

"I agree, but maybe something else is going on."

"Wait. Don't go alone. If you give me ten minutes, I'll go with you. I want to meet this guy."

Having Kat might help keep her emotions in check, and having a friend for support would be nice. "Alright, but please hurry. I don't know what's going on."

Once they arrived at the hospital, they made their way to Tom's room. Alyssa peeked inside and breathed a sigh of relief. No sign of Mrs. Chambers.

"Thanks for coming." Tom gazed at Alyssa, then glanced at Kat. Admiration sparked in his eyes. "Who's your friend?" He smiled and even sat up a little in bed.

Alyssa took a deep breath and blew it out. So much for his change of heart. He still had a wandering eye. "This is my roommate, Katarina."

He grinned at her friend. "Nice to meet you."

Kat glared at him and didn't say anything.

He shifted and cleared his throat.

"Tom, why did you call?" Alyssa didn't hide her irritation.

"I just didn't know what else to do. Emily called me. She sounded desperate, like she was in trouble."

"Why would she call you? Where is she? And why did you call me?" Alyssa lasered a look at him. "Why didn't you call the police?"

"I did call them."

"Then why am I here? I can't do anything."

"Yes, you can. Emily told me where she is."

"So, did you tell the police?"

Tom looked away. "No. Not really."

"What are you thinking? Emily, and whoever else is involved, has almost killed you."

"Twice." Kat held up two fingers.

"Emily didn't want the police involved," Tom said. "So, I told them most of what she said, but I left out the part about where she really is."

Alyssa took out her phone. "I'm calling the detective on the case. You need to tell the police, not me."

He shook his head. "I can't."

"You mean, you won't."

"I won't because I told Emily to come here, to my room. She's on her way." He held up a hand. "Before you say anything else, just listen. Her boyfriend has been the one behind everything, and she needed a safe place until the police catch him."

Kat growled. "You told a wanted fugitive to come to your room at the hospital?"

"She's not a fugitive; she's the victim." Tom gazed at Kat, then at Alyssa. "Emily needs our help."

"*Our* help?" Alyssa raised her hands in the air, then pointed at him. "She needs the police. Tom, I'm a nurse; this is a hospital where people come to get better, not be put in the middle of a crime scene."

"I know, but it's the best place for her to be. She can blend in here. Maybe you can let her put on some scrubs so nobody will know she's here."

"I knew I didn't like him." Kat crossed her arms and tapped her foot. "He's got bad vibes."

"I'm not the bad guy here. I'm trying to help. It'll be okay. I also called the private investigator. He's on his way to keep an eye on things."

Alyssa stepped closer to Tom's bedside. "By you calling me and telling me what you just did, you have made me an accessory in a crime. This is serious, Tom. I'm calling the detective whether you like it or not. I won't be part of this." Alyssa grabbed Kat by the arm. "Let's go."

"Wait," Tom called. "Please, don't leave."

"Tom, I should have left years ago." Alyssa turned, stepped out in the hall, and dialed the detective's number.

The call went to his voice mail, and she left a message.

"I'm proud of you," Kat said. "You stood tall and did the right thing."

"I'm so mad right now." Alyssa walked down the hall to the elevators as her friend stayed in pace with her. "I can't believe all of this. I just want Tom to go away."

Kat nodded. "Once the police get here, he's going to have some explaining to do."

"Definitely." The elevator arrived, they both stepped inside, and Alyssa punched the first-floor button. "Let's drop by the security office so I can let them know what's going on." As the elevator doors were closing, Alyssa glanced down the hall. A woman in scrubs, who looked very much like Emily Kingston, turned down Tom's hall.

Alyssa punched buttons, trying to get the elevator doors to open; it was too late; they were already on their way to the first floor. She mashed the next floor button and turned to her friend. "I think I saw Emily. We've got to get back up there."

As sickening sweet, gentle music played overhead, the elevator continued to pass the next floor, and the next, and the next, and didn't stop until they reached the bottom floor. Alyssa felt like pounding on the walls. When did an elevator keep going?

When the elevator finally stopped, the doors opened, and they had to wait as a nurse wheeled in a patient.

After what seemed an eternity, they finally reached the proper floor. Hurrying to Tom's room, Alyssa opened the door.

Emily, dressed in scrubs, stood next to Tom's bed.

Twenty-four

What was she supposed to do? Alyssa paused. Tried to process.

Tom gave her a sheepish grin. "Alyssa, this is Emily."

Emily, eyes red-rimmed, gazed her way. "I believe we've already met. Thank you for telling me what you did at the gas station. I didn't know what was going on."

"Why should we believe you?" Alyssa moved closer to the woman. "How could you not know?"

"David was the one behind everything," Tom said.

Emily nodded, hugged her arms around herself. "David told me he was filming a scene for a new movie and that he'd hired someone to video from the hill above my cabin. I didn't know it was Tom. I didn't even know he crashed." Her lip quivered, and she glanced at Tom. "David had hired an actor to pretend I was being attacked; then the guy drove me away from the back of the cabin on a snowmobile to another cabin about a mile away. I've been without cell service, TV, or internet and didn't know anything until you told me that Tom was here and had gotten hurt."

"But you were here in Boise. I saw you. Why didn't you contact the police?"

"The day you saw me was because David had to do something in town. I didn't know what happened, even then. David said he had heard rumors I was in danger, and he was keeping me isolated to keep me safe. He even took my phone."

"She was a prisoner." Tom reached for Emily's hand. She accepted his offer and sat in the chair next to his bed. "She finally got away from him when he left to run an errand. He doesn't know she's gone."

"He probably knows by now." Emily shuddered.

Still not convinced, Alyssa surveyed her. She did look scared. "How did you get away?"

"When I started piecing together what had happened and asking questions, David got really weird and scary." Tears pooled then ran down her face. "He started yelling and screaming, accusing me of all sorts of terrible things. Once he left, I ran to the house next door and asked to use their phone."

Alyssa reigned in her emotions. Was Emily acting? How could you tell if an actor wasn't acting? Was she being truthful, or was this all part of some wicked game?

Emily's eyes were pleading. "I know it sounds like a script from a bad movie, but I'm telling the truth. I need a safe place away from

David."

"You should have contacted the police and told them what happened."

"I know. I agree. I just needed to make sure Tom was okay. I needed to see a friendly face." Emily caressed Tom's chin.

The door slammed open. "You ungrateful witch." A dark-haired man pointed a gun at Emily. The same guy Alyssa had seen at the gas station.

The man moved closer to Emily. "After all I've done for you. I *made* you! You wouldn't have had a career if it wasn't for me."

Emily blanched, stood, backed against the wall. "You're crazy, David."

The man's pupils were huge, dilated. He waved the gun back and forth. "Back away, all of you."

Blood whooshing in her veins, Alyssa grabbed Kat and pulled her next to the wall out of his reach. Gaining courage, Alyssa stepped toward him. "The police are on their way."

David lasered a seething look at her. "They'll be too late." Keeping his gun aimed their way, he reached in his pocket with his free hand.

Lunging toward Emily, he plunged a syringe into her arm. "If I can't have you..." David's gaze flicked, burned, toward Tom. "no one can."

Emily's eyes rolled back in her head, and she crumbled to the floor.

Skin pebbling, Alyssa prayed for help,

prayed for strength. She needed to do something.

"Stay back!" He kept the gun pointed their way.

Emily groaned. She was still alive.

Turning toward Tom, David pulled another syringe out of his coat jacket. "Now, it's your turn."

Trying to shield himself, Tom screamed and held up his good arm, fighting as best he could.

Alyssa couldn't just stand there. Heart thumping, hoping David wouldn't notice, Alyssa took a small step forward.

Shoving Alyssa aside, Kat smacked David with a kick to the side of his head. The gun and syringe flew out of his hands, and with a groan, he crumpled to the floor.

Alyssa forced her mouth to close as she stared at her friend. "How did you do that?"

Kat grinned. "I do more than poetry when you're at work. Plus, when I'm away on the weekends visiting family, I train at my brother's martial arts studio. I'm also a black belt."

"Wow, thank you." Tom just about drooled as he surveyed Kat. I don't know what would have happened if you hadn't come in."

Alyssa ignored him, pushed the nurse's call button, and went to check Emily. Her breathing was shallow, but she was still alive. "Kat, check David's pockets. We need to find out what he gave her."

Kat pulled a vial out of David's pocket and

read the label.

Alyssa took a deep breath. Emily would be okay. The drug was only to render someone unconscious.

The door opened again, and the detective hurried into the room, grabbed David, pulled him to his feet, and handcuffed him. He glanced toward Emily and then at Alyssa. "Is she going to be okay?"

"Yes, she should be fine."

"Good." The detective scanned the room. "I will need statements from all of you."

Carla, one of the men from hospital security, and Tom's investigator, rushed inside the already crowded room.

The detective addressed Carla. "Take Emily somewhere she can stay under observation until I find out what happened."

Two hours later, after a lengthy debriefing by the police, hospital security, the private investigator, and filling in the curious nursing staff, Alyssa hugged Kat and walked her to the elevators. "Thanks for being here for me. I don't know what I would have done."

"You'd have handled things just fine, but I must admit I enjoyed taking down a bad guy." Kat made a ninja-like move.

"So, are you going to write a poem about what happened?"

"Of course. It's not often I have such fun material to work with. Who knows, maybe I'll write another book."

"*Another* book? I didn't know you had anything published."

Kat shrugged, and her mischievous smile lit her eyes. "I use an alias, a different name when I publish." With a wave, Kat stepped into the elevator. "There's so very much you don't know."

As the doors closed, Alyssa could have sworn she heard an adventure movie theme song playing.

A few minutes later, she made her way to the floor where she would be working for the night.

"Alyssa, I am glad that is over." Carla directed her to the nurse's station. "You sure do know how to get the blood pumping. What a wild way to start the shift."

"I'm just grateful everything turned out okay. Which reminds me, is Emily going to be alright?"

"Yes, she's already alert and talking to the police."

"That's good news. But man, what a mess she and her boyfriend made. I'm not sure if she was a victim or played a willing part in what happened."

"I'm sure the police will get all of that figured out. Do you want me to assign another nurse to Tom? Looks like he will be with us for a few more days."

"No, it's okay. I can handle him. I finally have closure on our relationship. Feels good to get past the past."

"Good for you." Carla laid her hand on Alyssa's shoulder. "You know I'm here if you need anything."

"Thanks. I appreciate all your help, but I will be glad when things get a little more normal."

"Good luck on that one." Carla chuckled and went back to her desk.

Alyssa made her rounds and couldn't believe all that had happened in the last few weeks.

She opened the door to Tom's room.

He smiled as she entered. "I was hoping I'd get to see you again. Thank you again for all you did."

"You're welcome. I'm grateful everything turned out okay."

"Yeah, me too. With any luck, I'll be out of here in a few days and back to California." He paused, his gaze catching hers. "Alyssa, I'm sorry again about the way I treated you. I hope you find someone who treats you the way you deserve."

"Thanks. I have."

"Good, I guess." He paused, his eyes surveying her." I'd say keep in touch, but I doubt you'd want that after everything that happened."

"I think we're good to just get on with our lives. As crazy as everything was while you were here, it did give me closure."

He ran a hand through his hair. "I guess closure is good. Take care of yourself."

"I will. You too." Alyssa turned, walked out, closed his door, and smiled.

Twenty-five

Sean checked his schedule. He'd been away from Alyssa far too long, and still his flights kept him from seeing her. In a few days, he'd fly down to Boise and pick up a couple he'd met when he'd flown their granddaughter for medical treatment in Salt Lake.

The downside of this trip was that he'd fly from Sun Valley to Boise on an early morning flight, then turn around and fly right back and wouldn't have time to see Alyssa. Maybe he could drive down to see her after he returned. It'd be a quick trip, but texts and phone calls weren't the same.

He hated all the craziness she'd been through with Tom and his family, and hated he couldn't have been there for her. Fortunately, from their latest phone conversations, it sounded like Alyssa was finally, really over Tom.

Sean took a deep breath. Until she was back in his arms, until he could look in her beautiful face, he wouldn't be able to rest easy.

~~*~*

Morning sun warming her back, Alyssa sat in the Wright's gazebo by the river. She was grateful God had opened her eyes to see the truth about Tom and so many things.

"I bought you a cup of hot cocoa." Mrs. Wright handed her a steaming mug of deliciousness and sat next to her. "I'm sorry if my being curious is a problem, but now that it's been a few weeks, do you mind if I ask what happened with everyone involved in that Emily Kingston affair?"

"Well, David, Emily's boyfriend, was arrested on charges of kidnapping, attempted murder, and a long list of other unpleasant things. When they searched his home, they found information proving Tom's innocence and what really happened to Emily. Even with David's high-priced lawyers, I figure he won't be out of prison anytime soon. Thankfully, Tom wasn't charged with anything, but he did receive very stern warnings from the police. He's now back in California, and from what I hear, dating Emily."

"Did they ever explain how Emily was involved?"

Alyssa nodded. "It was all so strange. David was insanely jealous of Emily. He'd seen Tom and Emily talking a couple of times at a coffee shop. So, David concocted the whole thing to not only create publicity for Emily but permanently remove Tom."

Mrs. Wright's eyes went wide. "Goodness,

that's awful. People can do terrible things."

"That's for sure. I'm just glad it's over."

"Me too. Do you think they will call you to testify?"

"Maybe? I'm not sure." The thought made Alyssa's heart sink.

"If they do, I want you to know we are here for you. You know, it wasn't an accident you stopped by that day. God has a way of connecting his children."

Alyssa smiled. "He does cool things like that."

"Yes, he does. And guess what? Robert and I are heading to Sun Valley for a few days. We've rented a cabin to go snow skiing, and we want you to join us. You could probably use a vacation after all you've been through."

"Really? what a generous offer. That sounds nice, but I may have to work. What days?"

"It's just a quick trip. We leave Saturday morning and will return Monday morning."

Alyssa thought about her schedule at the hospital. The timing couldn't have been better, and who would want to pass up a fantastic offer like that? "I'd love to."

"It's a date. Can you meet us at the Boise airport at 7:00 Saturday morning?"

"The airport?"

"Yes, we chartered a private plane. Robert's not too keen on driving too far in the winter. Plus, it's such a quick flight; we can get there faster and have more time to play."

"Wow, thank you, that sounds wonderful. I can pack a suitcase and have everything in my car so I can leave from work. I haven't been skiing in three years. Not sure how good I'll be on the slopes, but it sounds like a great time. Thank you so much. I haven't had a getaway in forever. I can't believe this." Alyssa had to stop herself from continuing to babble, so she took a drink of her hot cocoa.

Mrs. Wright chuckled. "It's our pleasure. I wish we could do more for you after all you've been through."

~~*~*

The week flew by, and Saturday morning, Alyssa hurried toward the small jet. She kept looking around, hoping she would see Sean. During their last conversation, he had told her he would also be at the Boise airport this morning to fly some people he had met when working with the air medical flight company.

Alyssa was thrilled to have a mini vacation with the Wrights, but the trip would have been perfect if she had been flying off with Sean.

"Hello!" Mr. Wright stepped down the stairs to meet her. "We are so glad you could join us. Come on board."

Alyssa stepped inside the small plane and sat across the aisle from the couple. "I'm so excited. Thank you for this wonderful opportunity."

"We're thrilled you could join us. Here I got

you something." Mrs. Wright handed her a blue and white scarf. "I knitted this for you to keep you warm on the slopes."

"Thank you. Goodness, you guys spoil me rotten."

The sound of the plane's door shutting drew her attention.

The pilot turned toward her, and his mouth dropped open. "Alyssa?"

"Sean!" Alyssa squealed, jumped to her feet, and hugged him. "I've missed you so much." After a sweet and very much appreciated kiss, followed by several more kisses, she looked up at his handsome face. "Did you plan this trip?"

"No. I didn't even know you would be here."

"What?" She turned toward her friends. "Did you know about Sean and me?"

Mr. Wright laughed. "Well, we did put things together pretty quickly when you came into our lives. We had our suspicions about you two, which have been completely confirmed after that greeting you gave one another."

"Oh, this is the BEST day ever!" Alyssa felt like doing a happy dance. However, her lack of dance ability kept her from making a complete fool of herself.

"Sean, if you have the weekend free, we hope you will join us," Mr. Wright said.

"Really?" Sean shook Mr. Wright's hand. "Thank you. I do have time off after we arrive in Sun Valley."

Teary-eyed, Mrs. Wright smiled at Alyssa.

"You two are such a sweet pair. We met Sean when he flew our granddaughter for medical treatment in Salt Lake City. We instantly bonded when he asked if he could pray for us. After the flight, we spent several hours talking and praying together, and we've stayed in touch since then. When God brought you into our lives, we started putting together some comments made by Sean about the girl he was dating. And then, the night you called asking for prayers, everything came together."

"So, you planned this trip because of us?" Alyssa asked.

"Partly for you both and partly for us. We've wanted to get away and do some skiing."

Alyssa shook her head as though trying to clear her thoughts. "This is so amazing. Things like this happen in movies, not to me."

"Well, they really are happening. I hope this weekend is as good as you both would imagine."

"It's already blown me away. Thank you."

"Yes, thank you." Sean addressed the Wrights, then hugged Alyssa again. "I better get this plane off the ground."

Smiling so wide she thought her face would split open from joy, Alyssa sat and buckled in her seat. How could she have been given such an amazing gift? She silently thanked God over and over. Then she turned to thank her friends again. "Thank you both for everything. You'll never know how much this means to me."

"It's our pleasure and honor," Mrs. Wright

said.

Alyssa blinked, wiped away the happy tears. "Thank you, again. And, I'm sorry I've been so focused on what was happening with me; I have barely asked anything about you both. Is your granddaughter okay?"

"She's doing well now. Thank you for asking. It was a scary season, but Lord willing, she should be fine."

Sensing the subject wasn't one to continue, Alyssa stared out of the window as they flew east toward Sun Valley. Her life was traveling in a different direction than she had ever thought before. All the years she'd wasted with Tom, then worrying about the past, and worrying about her future, had all been a terrible use of time. If only she had known then what she knew now. How grateful she was that God's mercies are new every morning.

Snow covered the hills below, gleaming in the sunshine like they had been scrubbed clean. The verse came to mind, *Create in me a clean heart oh God and renew a right spirit within me.* That's what she wanted, needed, to be washed clean, given a new start, renewed by God's grace and mercy.

Closing her eyes but keeping her heart open, she silently prayed, asking God for his new beginning, for her joy to be renewed, and that she would keep her focus on God and stop worrying about what happened in the past so she could step into whatever God had planned for her future.

The plane dropped and shuddered as it hit an air pocket. She took a deep breath, checked to make sure her seat belt was tight, then continued praying. She had to trust the pilot in the cockpit and the Pilot who was above them all.

Sean's voice came over the speaker. "Sorry about the turbulence. I'm climbing higher, and we should have smooth sailing until we reach our destination."

Alyssa smiled. That was the key, climb higher. Keep her focus on God, trust him, stay firmly buckled into God, and enjoy the journey.

Later that evening, after checking in at a beautiful Condo, then skiing on the slopes, the four of them sat on an oversized couch in front of a roaring fire in a stone fireplace.

Alyssa's cheeks hurt from smiling all day, and her legs burned from using muscles on the ski slopes she hadn't used in years. She nestled closer to Sean. "Is this a dream?"

He put his arm around her and pulled her close. "I've been pinching myself all day. I can't believe we've had this time together."

Mr. Wright groaned. "I think I'm too old for this." An eyebrow arched, and his eyes sparkled with humor as he turned to his wife. "Go skiing she said. It will be fun, she said. It's only been ten years since we last skied; you'll do fine, she said."

Mrs. Wright laughed and swatted his arm. "Oh, stop with the complaining. You're making me laugh, which makes me hurt even more than I already hurt. We *are* too old for this."

Mr. Wright joined in the laughter. "Stop, honey; they'll figure out our ploy. That we brought them because we needed a nurse and a strong man to help us move after spending a day on the slopes."

Alyssa giggled. "Whatever the reason you brought us with you, we are grateful."

"Definitely grateful," Sean added. "Can I order a pizza for us? I don't think any of us have the energy to go out somewhere to eat or the strength to prepare something."

"I'll pay if you order," Mr. Wright said. "I don't think I could even pick up a phone to make a call."

"I know the number of a great place." Sean grabbed his phone. "Is everyone okay with a large pizza with the works?"

Everyone agreed, and Sean made the call.

Forty-five minutes later, they sat around the table enjoying dinner.

"I don't think I'll be skiing tomorrow." Mr. Wright grimaced. "I think I displaced my displacer and broke my breaker."

Mrs. Wright nodded. "I think I'll stay in with him tomorrow morning. To be honest, I think I may not be able to move until about noon. Are you two going to be okay without us?"

"Actually," Sean glanced at the couple. "If

you both wouldn't mind, I'd like to pick up Alyssa in the morning and drive her to see something." He turned to Alyssa. "If you are okay with that?"

She grinned. "You can drive me wherever you want to go."

Twenty-six

Even though his muscles were sore and he could barely move after yesterday's skiing, Sean couldn't stop smiling. The time spent on the slopes with Alyssa, then sitting around talking with her and the Wrights, had been incredible.

He finished his breakfast, guzzled a cup of coffee, and hurried to get ready. After he had left the Wright's condo, he'd spent the rest of the evening getting his place ready to show Alyssa. He hoped and prayed she would love the cabin and love the area as much as he did.

He stopped at the door and turned back to survey his place. The cabin still needed lots of work, but it was more than he could have imagined he would ever own at this time of his life. Now, if everything worked out, if his prayers were answered, Alyssa would be by his side as his wife.

~~*~*

"It's beautiful, Sean." Alyssa stood looking out the large window of the cabin. He'd given her the tour of the property and proudly showed her the cabin he'd purchased. She couldn't believe it was his.

He stood next to her and placed his arm around her shoulder. "You like it?"

She nestled against his strong side. "I love it. I know you always wanted a cabin by a river."

"You remembered?" His eyebrows raised.

"Yes. When we were kids, you always talked about your life goals. I envied that about you. You wanted to be a pilot and have a place like this."

"You had your dreams too."

Alyssa turned to face him. "I did?"

"You wanted to be a nurse. And, you reached that goal. Don't you remember the other thing you mentioned?"

She tried to think back, but nothing came to mind. "I don't think so."

Sean took her hand and led her to the couch and patted the cushion next to him. He waited until she sat. "Close your eyes."

She grinned and squeezed her eyes shut.

"Okay, I want you to think back. You'd just turned seventeen. It was your birthday, and you hadn't had a very good day."

Alyssa frowned, gulped as memories flooded back. She'd come home that day hoping her parents would have a birthday cake, or party, or something to celebrate, but all she had found was a note on the counter. Her parents had gone away together on a business trip. They hadn't even remembered her birthday. She looked over at him. "Sean, that's not a very good memory."

"I know. I'm sorry, but what happened next. Do you remember?"

She let out a sigh and closed her eyes again, trying to recall what happened next. Sean had come over with a bouquet of wildflowers he'd picked, and she'd fallen into his arms in tears. He held her close, let her cry, and then led her to the little stream that ran near their neighborhood. They'd sat for hours together, not saying much, just being together. Then, she remembered what she had said.

Alyssa opened her eyes again and looked at her friend, the little boy who had turned into the handsome man she loved. "Oh, Sean, I said I wanted to fly away, go somewhere far away, live in a cabin in the mountains by a river."

His gentle eyes surveyed her. "Do you remember what I told you?"

A lump formed in her throat as tears welled in her eyes. "You said you would always be there for me. That I would never be alone."

"I'm sorry I haven't done better. I want to make that promise true now."

He pulled a small velvet box out of his pocket, then slid down on one knee. "Alyssa Nelson, would you do me the honor of being my wife?"

She could have sworn her heart laughed with joy. "Yes, Sean Connery, I would love to be your wife."

Colorful spring flowers bloomed on the bank of the river. Alyssa sat on the Wright's deck and gazed at the engagement ring sparkling on her finger on her left hand. In twenty-six days, she'd become Mrs. Sean Connery. She giggled at the thought. Once they returned from their honeymoon in the Caribbean, they would live at the home he had bought, and she would start a new job at the area hospital.

"I brought you some lemonade." Mrs. Wright handed Alyssa a glass and sat next to her. "I can't wait for your wedding."

"Me neither."

"I really like Sean. He's such a fine young man and very handsome."

"Yes, he is. I can't believe how lucky I am. Not just lucky, blessed."

"I'm excited for you. I will miss you, though. I've enjoyed our time together."

"I'll miss you too. I'll be back from time to time, and you know you're always welcome to drive over and see us. It's not as nice as what you have, but it's perfect for the two of us." Alyssa showed her friend the photos she'd taken from her last visit to see Sean.

Mrs. Wright smiled wide. "Oh, it's perfect."

"Yes, absolutely perfect." Alyssa looked around her at the beauty of the world, the trees budding, the river running clear and beautiful. "I'm thankful for all God has done for me and very thankful he opened my eyes." She gazed over at her friend. "And, I'm thankful we met. Thank you for all your advice and prayers. You'll never know how much that meant."

"It was my pleasure and honor. Alyssa, as you step into this next phase in your life, keep watching how God is working. Watch for all he does, the people he brings into your life, and the opportunities he gives each day to be with him and be part of his amazing work in the world."

"That's a neat thought. I wonder, what if we lived with our spiritual eyes wide open so we could see what had been unnoticed and see beyond our earthly vision."

"Yes, it would be wonderful. In God's amazing reality, it's about seeing the unseen through the eyes of The One who sees all. It's about looking beyond the possible to see the impossible, to see the grandness of our Great God."

"I love that! Yes. But I guess that means I have to be open to look, watch, and acknowledge what the Lord has done and is doing."

"Yes." Mrs. Wright pointed to Alyssa's camera. "Just like the longer the lens is open, the more light comes in. The more time we spend with God, reading the Bible, and praying, the more God's light will shine. All around us, every day, every moment, God is working. God's handprints are all over creation; he paints his love in the sunrise and the sunsets, in the

gentle breeze, and in the flowers of the field."
Mrs. Wright placed her hand on her chest. "And,
every heartbeat we are given signals God's
continued purpose for our lives."

Alyssa nodded and sat quiet, looking at the
beauty God created around her, letting the
thoughts and words steep deep in her soul.
Whatever came next was bigger than her
relationship with Sean. Her life and her heart
were eternal and forever safe in the loving
hands of God.

She smiled, and in a silent prayer of
gratitude, gazed heavenward. *Heavenly Father,
thank you for all you have done for me. Thank
you for the ways you have worked and the many
ways you continue to work in my life. Thank
you for the people you have brought into my
path. Thank you for your forgiveness and for the
healing you have done for my past. Please open
my eyes to notice how You are working and to
view life from Your perfect perspective. Oh, how
I want to see beyond my earthly vision to notice
all You desire me to see. Thank you, God. I love
you. Thank you for loving me.*

The End.

Thank you for reading
Open Lens

Lisa Buffaloe

I realize not every story on earth ends with a happy ending. However, I do know One who gives an eternal, happy-ever-after. Jesus Christ loves like no other. He loves with an unfailing love, loving through the good, bad, and ugly of life. Christ tenderly beckons, "Come to Me, all who are weary and heavy-laden, and I will give you rest.... I am gentle and humble in heart, and you will find rest for your souls" (Matthew 11:28-29, NASB).

No matter what you have done, or what has been done to you, the mercy and grace of Jesus Christ waits to make all things new. For, "God loved the world so much that he gave his one and only Son so that whoever believes in him may not be lost, but have eternal life" (John 3:16, NCV). Christ died and rose again so that your heart could be filled with His love.

Your heart is home with Jesus, and He gives eternal security and rest for your heart, mind, and soul. He will never tire of you, and His love will never let go. You will never be alone and never forsaken. He promises, "I have loved you just as the Father has loved Me; remain in My love [and do not doubt My love for you]." For, "I have loved you with an everlasting love" (John 15:9, AMP, Jeremiah 31:3, NASB).

Just as Jesus placed his hands on the blind man's eyes and the man's sight was restored, and he then saw everything clearly (Mark 8:25). Go to the Savior, Jesus Christ, and let Him open your heart and your eyes.

Therefore, "[I pray] that the eyes of your heart [the very center and core of your being] may be enlightened [flooded with light by the Holy Spirit], so that you will know and cherish the hope [the divine guarantee, the confident expectation] to which He has called you, the riches of His glorious inheritance in the saints (God's people), and [so that you will begin to know] what the immeasurable and unlimited and surpassing greatness of His [active, spiritual] power is in us who believe. These are in accordance with the working of His mighty strength" (Ephesians 1:18-19, AMP).

"So, we fix our eyes not on what is seen, but on what is unseen, since what is seen is temporary, but what is unseen is eternal" (2 Corinthians 4:18, NIV).

"Now to Him who is able to do far more abundantly beyond all that we ask or think, according to the power that works within us, to Him be the glory in the church and in Christ Jesus to all generations forever and ever. Amen" (Ephesians 3:20-21, NASB).

About the Author

Lisa Buffaloe is a happily married mom, multi-published author, and speaker. She loves to encourage others that regardless of past or present situations in life, God's tender, unending love provides healing, restoration, renewal, and joy.

When Lisa's not writing, she enjoys long walks with her husband and exploring God's beautiful nature.

Visit Lisa at https://lisabuffaloe.com

Books by Lisa Buffaloe

(Updated July 2023)

Fiction

The Masterpiece Beneath
Nadia's Hope (Hope and Grace Series, Book 1)
  Prodigal Nights (Hope and Grace Series, 2)
  Writing Her Heart (Hope and Grace Series, 3)
   The Discovery Chapter (Hope and Grace Series, 4)
   Open Lens (Hope and Grace Series, 5)
The Fortune
Grace for the Char-Baked

Non-Fiction

Float by Faith
Heart and Soul Medication
Time with The Timeless One
The Forgotten Resting Place
Present in His Presence
We Were Meant for Paradise
One Lit Step: Devotions for your journey
The Unnamed Devotional
Flying on His Wings
Unfailing Treasures
No Wound Too Deep for The Deep Love of Christ
Living Joyfully Free Devotional, (Volume 1)
Living Joyfully Free Devotional, (Volume 2)

"I ask—ask the God of our Master, Jesus Christ, the God of glory—to make you intelligent and discerning in knowing him personally, your eyes focused and clear, so that you can see exactly what it is he is calling you to do, grasp the immensity of this glorious way of life he has for his followers, oh, the utter extravagance of his work in us who trust him—endless energy, boundless strength!" (Ephesians 1:18, MSG).

Acknowledgments

I gratefully thank my Lord and Savior, Jesus Christ, for Your forgiveness, grace, and mercy. Thank You, Heavenly Father, for gifting me with the words to write this novel. May You be honored and glorified, and may my eyes be open to see the beauty of Your unfailing love.

I gratefully thank my sweet husband for allowing me time to write. I love you and am so very grateful God brought us together.

A BIG thank you to those who have provided encouragement for my writing journey and to those who have taken the time to read this book. Thank you.

I also gratefully thank each Bible publisher for the use of the scripture quotations.

Scripture quotations taken from the New American Standard Bible®, NASB), Copyright © 1960, 1962, 1963, 1968, 1971, 1972, 1973, 1975, 1977, 1995 by The Lockman Foundation Used by permission. www.Lockman.org

Scripture quotations taken from the Amplified® Bible (AMP), Copyright © 2015 by The Lockman Foundation Used by permission. www.Lockman.org

Scripture taken from the New Century Version® (NCV). Copyright © 2005 by Thomas Nelson, Inc. Used by permission. All rights reserved.

THE HOLY BIBLE, NEW INTERNATIONAL VERSION®, NIV® Copyright © 1973, 1978, 1984, 2011 by Biblica, Inc.™ Used by permission. All rights reserved worldwide.

Open Lens

A novel

Lisa Buffaloe

www.ingramcontent.com/pod-product-compliance
Lightning Source LLC
Chambersburg PA
CBHW051512170626
46811CB00002B/790